Leerie

Ruth Sawyer

Alpha Editions

This edition published in 2022

ISBN : 9789356716636

Design and Setting By
Alpha Editions
www.alphaedis.com
Email - info@alphaedis.com

As per information held with us this book is in Public Domain.
This book is a reproduction of an important historical work. Alpha Editions uses the best technology to reproduce historical work in the same manner it was first published to preserve its original nature. Any marks or number seen are left intentionally to preserve its true form.

Contents

Foreword .... - 1 -

Chapter I .... - 3 -

    THE MAN WHO FEARED SLEEP .... - 3 -

Chapter II .... - 19 -

    OLD KING COLE .... - 19 -

Chapter III .... - 35 -

    THE CHANGELING .... - 35 -

Chapter IV .... - 53 -

    FOR THE HONOR OF THE SAN .... - 53 -

Chapter V .... - 70 -

    THE LAST OF THE SURGICAL .... - 70 -

Chapter VI .... - 86 -

    MONSIEUR SATAN .... - 86 -

Chapter VII .... - 104 -

    THE LAD WHO OUTSANG THE STARS .... - 104 -

Chapter VIII .... - 120 -

INTO HER OWN ....- 120 -
AFTERWORD..- 137 -

Foreword

I LIKE to write stories. Best of all I like to write stories about people who help the world to go round with a little more cheer and good will than is usual. You know—and I know—there are a few who put into life something more than the bare ingredients. They add a plum here—extra spice there. They bake it well—and then they trim it up like an all-the-year-round birthday cake with white frosting, angelica, and red cherries. Last of all they add the candles and light them so that it glows warmly and invitingly for all; fine to see, sweet to taste.

Of course, there are not so many people with the art or the will to do this, and, having done it, they have not always the bigness of heart to pass it round for the others to share. But I like to make it my business to find as many as I can; and when I am lucky enough to find one I pop him—or her—into a book, to have and to hold always as long as books last and memory keeps green.

Not long ago I was ill—ridiculously ill—and my doctor popped me into a sanitarium. "Here's the place," I said, "where people are needed to make the world go round cheerfully, if they are needed anywhere." And so I set about to get well and find one.

She came—before I had half finished. The first thing I noticed was the inner light in her—a light as from many candles. It shone all over her face and made the room brighter for a long time after she had left. The next thing I noticed was the way everybody watched for her to come round—everybody turning child again with nose pressed hard against the window-pane. It made me remember Stevenson's *Lamplighter*; and for many days there rang in my ears one of his bits of human understanding:

> And oh! before you hurry by with ladder and with light,
> O Leerie, see a little child and nod to him to-night.

Before I knew it I had all the makings of a story. I trailed it through the mud of gossip and scandal; I followed it to the highroad of adventure and on to the hills of inspiration and sacrifice. It was all there—ripe for the plucking; and with the good assistance of Hennessy I plucked it. Before the story was half written I was well—so much for the healing grace of a story and the right person to put in it.

This much I have told that you may know that *Leerie* is as true as all the best and finest things in the world are true. I am only the passer-on of life as she has made it—spiced, trimmed, and lighted with many candles. So if the taste pleases, help yourself bountifully; there is enough for all. And if you must thank any one—thank *Leerie*.

RUTH SAWYER.

Chapter I

THE MAN WHO FEARED SLEEP

PETER BROOKS felt himself for a man given up. He had felt his physical unfitness for some time in the silent, condemning judgment masked under the too sympathetic gaze of his fellow-men; he had felt it in the over-solicitous inquiries after his health made by the staff; and there was his chief, who had fallen into the comfortable week-end habit of telling him he looked first-rate, and in the same breath begging him to take the next week off. For months past he had been conscious of the sidelong glances cast by his brother alumni at the College Club when he appeared, and the way they had of dropping into a contradictory lot of topics whenever he joined a group unexpectedly showed only too plainly that he had been the real subject under discussion. Yes, he felt that the world at large had turned its thumb down as far as he was concerned, but it had caused him surprisingly little worry until that last visit to Doctor Dempsy.

There it was as if Peter's sensibilities concerning himself had suddenly become acute. The doctor sounded too reassuring even for a combined friend and physician; he protested too much that he had found nothing at all the matter with him—nothing at all. When a doctor seems so superlatively anxious to set a man right with himself, it is time to look out; therefore the casual, just-happened-to-mention-it way that he finally broached the question of a sanitarium came within an inch of knocking the last prop from under Peter's resolve not to lose his grip. For the first time he fully realized how it felt to be given up, and, characteristically, he thanked the Almighty that there was no one to whom it would really matter.

For a year he had been slowly going to pieces; for a year he had been dropping in for Dempsy to patch him up. There had been a host of miserable puny ailments which in themselves meant nothing, but combined and in a young man meant a great deal. Of late his memory had failed him outrageously; he had had frequent attacks of vertigo, and these of themselves had rendered him unreliable and unfit for newspaper work. Irresponsible! Unfit! Peter snorted the words out honestly to himself. Under these conditions, and with no one to care, he could see no plausible reason for trying to coax a mere existence out of life.

To those who knew him best—to Doctor Dempsy most of all—his condition seemed unexplainable. Here was a man who never drank, who never overfed, who smoked in moderation, whose life stood out conspicuously decent and clean against the possibilities of his environment. What lay back of this going to pieces? Doctor Dempsy had tried for a year to find out and had failed. To Peter, it was not unexplainable at all—he knew. Possessed of a constitution above the average, he had forced it to do the work of a mind far above the average, while he had denied it one of the three necessities of life and sanity. His will and reason had been powerless to help him—and now?

Because he had hated himself for hiding this knowledge from the man who had tried to do so much for him and wanted to make amends in some way—and because it was the easiest thing, after all, to agree—he let Doctor Dempsy pick out a sanitarium, make all arrangements, buy his ticket, and see him off. He drew the line at being personally conducted, however. Whether he went to a sanitarium or not did not matter; what mattered was how long would he stay and where would he go afterward. Or would there be an afterward? These were the questions that mulled through Peter's mind on the train, and, coupled with the memory of the worried kindliness on Doctor Dempsy's face, they were the only traveling companions Peter had. It was not to be wondered, therefore, that as he left the car and boarded the sanitarium omnibus he felt indescribably old, weary, and finished with things.

At first he thought he was the only passenger, but as the driver leisurely gathered up his reins and gave a cluck to the horses a girl's voice rang out from the station, "Flanders—Flanders! Why, I believe you're forgetting me." And the next instant the girl herself appeared, suitcase in hand.

The driver grinned down a sheepish apology and Peter turned to hold the door open. She stood framed in the doorway for a moment while she lifted in her case, and for that moment Peter had conflicting impressions. He was conscious of a modest, nun-like appearance of clothes; the traveling-suit was gray, and the small gray hat had an encircling breast of white feathers. The lips had a quiet, demure curve; but the chin was determined, almost aggressive, while the gray eyes positively emitted sparks. The girl was not beautiful, she was luminous—and all the gray clothing in the world could not quench her. Peter found himself instantly wondering how anything so vitally alive and fresh to look at could be headed for a sanitarium with broken-down hulks like himself.

She caught Peter's eye upon her and smiled. "If Flanders will hurry we'll be there in time to see Hennessy feeding the swans," she announced.

There was no response. Peter had suddenly lost the knack of it, along with other things. He could only look bewildered and a trifle more tired. But the girl must have understood it was only a temporary lack, for she did not draw in like a snail and dismiss Peter from her conscious horizon. She smiled again.

"I see. Newcomer?" And, nodding an affirmative to herself, she went sociably on: "Hennessy and the swans are symbolical. Couldn't tell you why—not in a thousand years—but you'll feel it for yourself after you've been here long enough. Hennessy hasn't changed in fifteen years—maybe longer for those who can reckon longer. Same old blue jumper, same old tawny corduroys; if he ever had a new pair he's kept them to himself. And the swans have changed less than Hennessy. If anything gets on your nerves here—treatment, doctors, nurses, anything—go and watch Hennessy. He's the one sure, universal cure."

The bus swung round the corner and brought the ivy-covered building into sight. The girl's face grew lighter and lighter; in the shadow of the bus it seemed to Peter actually to shine. "Dear old San," she said under her breath. "Heigh-ho! it's good to get back!"

Before Peter could fathom any reason for this unaccountable rejoicing, the bus had stopped and the girl and suitcase had vanished. Wearily he came back to his own reason for being there, and docilely he allowed the porter to shoulder his luggage and conduct him within.

Three days passed—three days in which Peter thought little and felt much. He had been passed about among the staff of doctors very much like a delectable dish, and sampled by all. Half a dozen had taken him in hand. He had been apportioned a treatment, a diet, a bath hour, and a nurse. Looking back on those three days—and looking forward to a continuous protraction of the same—he could see less reason than ever for coaxing an existence out of life. Life meant to him work—efficient, telling work—and companionship—sharing with a congenial soul recreation, opinions, and meals—and some day, love. Well—what of these was left him? It was then that he remembered the gray girl's advice in the omnibus and went out to find Hennessy and the swans.

His nurse was at supper, so he was mercifully free; moreover it was the emptiest time of day for out-of-doors. A few straggling patients were knocking prescribed golf-balls about the links, and a scattering of nurses were hurrying in with their wheel-chairs. Half-way between the links and the last building was the pond, shaded by pines and flanked by a miniature rustic rest-house, and thither Peter went. On a willow stump emerging from the pond he found Hennessy, as wrinkled as a butternut, with a thatch of gray hair, a mouth shirred into a small, open ellipse, and eyes full of irrepressible twinkles. He was seated tailor fashion on the stump, a tin platter of bread across his knees and the swans circling about him. He looked every whit as Irish as his name, and he was scolding and blarneying the birds by turn.

"Go-wan, there, ye feathered heathen! Can't ye be lettin' them that has good manners get a morsel once in a while? Faith, ye'll be havin' old Doc Willum afther ye with his stomach cure if ye don't watch out." He looked over his shoulder and caught Peter's gaze. "Sure, birds or humans, they all have to be coaxed or scolded into keepin' healthy, I'm thinkin', and Hennessy's head nurse to the swans," he ended, with a chuckle.

But there was something quite different on Peter's mind. "Has one of the patients—a young person in gray—been here lately? I mean have you seen her about any time?"

Hennessy shook a puzzled head. "A young gray patient, ye say? Sure there might be a hundred—that's not over-distinguishin'. I leave it to ye, sir, just a gray patient is not over-distinguishin'."

Peter reflected. "It was a quiet, cloister kind of gray, but her eyes were not—cloistered. They were the shiningest—"

A chuckle from Hennessy brought him to an abrupt finish. "Eyes? Gray? Patient? Ha, ha! Did ye hear that, Brian Boru?" and he flicked his cap at a gray swan. "Sure, misther, that's no patient. 'Tis Leerie—herself."

"Leerie?" The name sounded absurd to Peter, and slightly reminiscent of something, he could not tell what.

"Aye, Leerie. Real name, Sheila O'Leary—as good a name as Hennessy. But they named her Leerie her probation year. In course she's Irish an' not Scotch, an' I never heard tell of a lass afore that went 'round a-lightin' street lamps, but for all that the name fits. Ye mind grown-ups an' childer alike watch for her to come 'round."

"A nurse," repeated Peter, dully.

"Aye. An' she come back three days since, Heaven be praised! afther bein' gone three years."

"Three years," repeated Peter again. "Why was she gone three years?"

Hennessy eyed him narrowly for a moment. "A lot of blitherin' fools sent her away, that's what, an' she not much more than graduated. Suspension, they called it."

"Suspension for what?"

The shirring in Hennessy's lips tightened, and he drew his breath in and out in a sort of asthmatic whistle. This was the only sign of emotion ever betrayed by Hennessy. When he spoke again he fairly whistled his words.

"If ye want to know what for—ye can ask some one else. Good night." And with a bang to the platter Hennessy was away before Peter could stop him.

Alone with the swans, Peter lingered a moment to consider. A nurse. The gray person a nurse! And sent away for some—some—Peter's mind groped inadequately for a reason. Pshaw! He could smile at the absurdity of his interest. What did it matter—or she matter—or anything matter? For a man who has been given up, who has been sent away to a sanitarium to finish with life as speedily and decently as he can, to stand on one leg by a pond, for all the world like a swan himself, and wonder about a girl he had seen but once, in a sanitarium omnibus, was absurd. And the name Leerie? Of course they had taken it from Stevenson, but it suited. Yes, Hennessy was right, it certainly suited.

A rustle of white skirts coming down the path attracted his attention. It was his nurse, through supper, coming like a commandant to take him in charge. Thirty-seven, in a sanitarium, with a nurse attendant! Peter groaned inwardly. It was monstrous, a cowardly, blackguard attack of an unthinking Creator on a human being—a decent human being—who might be—who wanted to be—of some use in the world. For a breath he wanted to roar forth blasphemy after blasphemy against the universe and its Maker, but in the next breath he suddenly realized how little he cared. With a smile almost tragically senile, he let the nurse lead him away.

And all the while a girl was leaning over the sill of the little rest-house, watching him. It was a girl with a demure mouth, a determined chin, and eyes that shone, who answered impartially to the names of Sheila, Miss O'Leary, or Leerie. The gray was changed for the white uniform and cap of a graduate nurse, and the change was becoming. She had recognized him at first with casual amusement as she watched him fill her prescription of Hennessy and the swans, but after Hennessy had gone she watched him with all the intuitive sympathy of her womanhood and the understanding of her profession. Not one of the emotions that swept Peter's face but registered full on the girl's sensibilities: the illuminating interest in something, bewilderment, hopelessness, despair, agony, and a final weary surrender to the inevitable—they were all there. But it was the strange, haunting look in the deep-set eyes that made the girl sit up, alert and curious.

"'Phobia,'" she said, softly, under her breath. "Not over-fed liver or alcoholic heart, but 'phobia, I'll wager, poor childman! Wonder how the doctors have diagnosed him!"

She learned how a few days later when Miss Maxwell, the superintendent of nurses, stopped her in the second-floor corridor. "My dear, I should like to change you from Madam Courot to another case for a few days. Miss Jacobs is on now and—"

"Coppy?" Sheila O'Leary broke in abruptly, a smile of amusement breaking the demureness of her lips. "Needn't explain, Miss Max. I see. Young male patient, unattached. Frequent pulse-takings and cerebral massage, with late evening strolls in the pine woods. Business office takes notice and a change of nurse recommended. Poor Coppy—ripping nurse! If only she wouldn't grow flabby every time a pair of masculine eyes are focused her way!"

"But it wasn't the business office this time." Miss Maxwell herself smiled as she made the statement. "It was the patient himself. He asked for a change."

"A man that's a man for all he's a patient. God bless his soul!" and a look of sudden radiant delight swept the girl's face. "What's he here for? Jilting chorus-girl—fatty degeneration of his check-book?"

The superintendent shook her head. "He doesn't happen to be that kind. He's a newspaper-man—a personal friend of Doctor Dempsy's. Overwork, he thinks, and for a year he's been trying to put him back on his feet. It's a case of nerves, with nothing discoverable back of it so far as he can see, but he wants us to try. Doctor Nichols has analyzed him; teeth have been X-rayed; eyes, nose, and throat gone over. There's nothing radically wrong with stomach or kidneys; heart shows nervous affection, nothing more. He ought to be fit physically and he isn't. Miss Jacobs reports a maximum of an hour's sleep in twenty-four. Doctor Dempsy writes it's a case for a nurse, not a doctor, and the most tactful, intuitive nurse we have in the sanitarium. Please take it, Leerie."

The girl stiffened under the two hands placed on her shoulders, while something indescribably baffling and impenetrable took possession of her whole being. Her voice became almost curt. "Sorry, can't. Bargain, you know. Wouldn't have come back at all if you hadn't promised I should not be asked to take those cases."

"I'll not ask you to take another, but you know how I feel about any patient Doctor Dempsy sends to us. Anything I can do means paying back a little on the great debt I owe him, the debt of a wonderful training. That's why I ask—this once." A look almost fanatical came into the face of the superintendent.

The girl smiled wistfully up at her. "Wish I could! Honest I do, Miss Max! I'd fight for the life of any patient under the old San roof—man, woman, or child; but I'll not baby-tend unhealthy-minded young men. You know as well as I how it's always been: they lose their heads and I my temper—results, the same. I end by telling them just what I think; they pay their bills and leave the same day. The San loses a perfectly good annual patient, and the business office feels sore at me. No, I'm no good at frequent pulses and cerebral massage; leave that to Coppy."

There was no stinging sarcasm in the girl's voice. She reached out an impulsive hand and slipped it into one of the older woman's, leaving it there long enough to give it a quick, firm grip. "Remember, it's only three years—and it takes so little to set tongues wagging again. So let's stick fast to the bargain, dear; only nervous old ladies or the bad surgical cases."

"Very well. Only—if you could change your mind, let me know. In the mean time I'll put Miss Saunders on," and the superintendent turned away, troubled and unsatisfied.

An hour later Sheila O'Leary came upon Miss Saunders with her new patient, and the patient was the man of the omnibus—the man with the haunting, deep-set eyes. Unnoticed, she watched them sitting on a bench by the pond, the nurse droning aloud from a book, the man sagging listlessly, plainly hearing nothing and seeing nothing. The picture set Sheila O'Leary shuddering. If it was a case of 'phobia, God help the poor man with Saunders coupled to his nerves! Cumbersome, big-hearted, and hopelessly dull, Saunders was incapable of nursing with tactful insight a nerve-racked man. In the whole wide realm of disease there seemed nothing more tragic to Sheila than a victim of 'phobia. It turned normal men and women into pitiful children, afraid of the dark, groping out for the hand to reassure them, to put heart and courage back in them again—the hand that nine cases out of ten never reaches them in time.

With an impulsive toss of her head, Sheila O'Leary swung about in her tracks. She would break her own bargain for this once. She would go to Miss Max and ask to be put on the case. Here was a soul sick unto death with a fear of something, and Saunders was nursing it! What did it matter if it was a man or a dog, as long as she could get into the dark after him and show him the way out! Her resolve held to the point of branching paths, and there she stopped to consider again.

Peter's eyes were on the swans; there was nothing to the general droop of the shoulders, the thrust-forward bend of the neck, the hollowing of the smooth-shaven cheeks, and the graying of the hair above the temples to write him other than an average overworked or habitually harassed business man here for rest and treatment. If Sheila was mistaken—if there was no abnormal mental condition back of it all, no legitimate reason for not holding fast to the compact she had made three years before with herself to leave men—young, old, or middle-aged—out of her profession, what a fool she would feel! She balanced the paths and her judgment for a second, then decided in favor of the bargain. So Peter was left to the ministrations of Saunders.

That night the unexpected happened, unexpected as far as the sanitarium, the superintendent of nurses, and Sheila O'Leary were concerned. How unexpected it was to Peter depends largely on whether it was the result of a decision on his part to stop coaxing existence—or a desire to escape permanently from Saunders—or merely an accident. However, Sheila O'Leary was called in the middle of the night, when she was sleeping so soundly that it took the combined efforts of the superintendent and the head night nurse to shake her awake. As she hurried into her uniform they gave her the bare details. Somehow the doors of the sun-parlor had not been fastened as usual, and a patient had stayed up there after lights were out. He had tried to find his way to the lift, had slipped the fastenings of the door in his effort to locate the bell, and had fallen four stories, to the top of the lift itself. The whole accident was unbelievable, unprecedented. They might find some plausible explanation in the morning—but in the mean time the patient was in the operating-room and Sheila O'Leary was to report at once for night duty.

As the girl pinned on her cap the superintendent whispered the last instructions: "You'll find him in Number Three, Surgical. It's one of your fighting cases, Leerie, and it's Doctor Dempsy's patient. Remember, your best work this time, girl, for all our sakes!"

And it was a fighting case. Innumerable nights followed, all alike. The temperature rose and fell a little, only to rise again; the pulse strengthened and weakened by turns; delirium continued unbroken. As night after night wore on and no fresh sign of internal injury developed, the girl found herself forgetting the immediate condition of the patient and going back to the thing that had brought him here. If she was right and he was possessed by a fixed idea, the dread of some concrete thing or experience, his delirium showed no evidence. It seemed more the delirium of exhaustion than fever, and there was no raving. Consciousness, however, might reveal what delirium hid, so, as the nights slipped monotonously by, the girl found herself waiting with a growing eagerness for the man to come back to himself.

The waiting seemed interminable, but a time came at last when Sheila slipped through the door of No. 3 and found a pair of deep-set, haunting eyes turned full upon her.

"It's—it's Leerie." The words came with some difficulty, but there was an untold relief in Peter's voice.

For a moment the girl was taken aback, but only for a moment. She laughed him a friendly little laugh while she put her hand down to the hand that was still too weak to reach out in greeting. "Yes. Oh yes, it's Leerie. Been getting pretty well acquainted with you these weeks, but rather a surprise to find it so—so mutual."

"I got acquainted with you—beforehand," announced Peter.

"I see—omnibus, Hennessy, and the swans." She laughed again softly. "You've been away a long time; hope you're glad to get back."

Peter reflected. "I'm afraid I'm not. But I'll not say it if it sounds too much like a quitter."

"No, say it and get it out of your system. Getting well always seems a terrible undertaking; and the stronger you've been the harder it seems." Sheila turned to her chart and preparations for the night.

Lights out, she sat down by the open window to wait for Peter to sleep. An hour passed, two hours, and sleep did not come. She fed him hot milk and he still lay open-eyed, almost rigid, staring straight at the ceiling. At midnight she stole out for her own supper in the diet-kitchen and found him still awake when she returned, the haunting eyes looking more child's than man's in the dimness of the night lamp. Had she been free to follow her most vagrant impulse, she would have climbed on the head of the bed, taken the bandaged head on her lap, and plunged into the most enthralling tale of boy adventure her imagination could compass. But she hounded off the impulse, after the fashion of treating all vagrants, and went back to the window to wait and wonder. Peter was still awake when the gray of the morning crept down the corridors of the Surgical.

Sheila questioned Tyler, the day nurse, as she came off duty the next evening, "Number Three sleep any to boast of?"

"Why, no! Didn't he sleep well last night?"

She gave a non-committal shrug and passed into the room. He was watching for her coming, and a ghost of a smile flickered at the corners of his mouth. She couldn't remember having seen even so much of a smile before.

"It's—it's Leerie." He said it just as he had the night before. But there was a strange, wistful appeal in the voice which set Sheila wondering afresh.

"Gorgeous night, full of stars, and air like wine. Smell the verbena and thyme from the San gardens?" Sheila threw back her head and sniffed the air like a wild thing. "Took me a month to trail that smell—be sure of it.

You only get it at night after a light rain. Take some long breaths of it and you'll be asleep before lights are out."

But he was not. He lay rigid as the night before, his eyes staring straight before him. Sheila remembered a description she had read once of a mountain guide who had been caught on the edge of a landslide and hung for hours over the abyss, clutching a half-felled tree and trying to keep awake until help came. The man she was nursing might almost be living through such an agony of mind and body, afraid to yield up his consciousness lest he should go plunging off into some horrible abyss. What did he fear? Was it sleep? Was somnophobia what lay behind the wrecking of this fine, clean manhood? The thing seemed incredible, and yet—and yet—

Before dawn crept again into the Surgical, the mind of Sheila O'Leary was made up. Peter was suddenly aware that the nurse was close at his bedside, chafing the clenched fingers free. It was that mysterious hour that hangs between the going night and coming day, the most non-resisting time for body and mind, when the human will gives up the struggle if it gives it up at all. And Sheila O'Leary, being well aware of this, rubbed the tense nerves into a comfortable state of relaxation and talked.

First she talked of the city, and found he was not city-born. Then she talked of the country—of South, East, and West—and located his birthplace in a small New England village. She talked of the outdoor freedom of a country boy, of the wholesome work and fun on a farm with a large family and good old-fashioned parents, and she found that he had been an only child, motherless, with a family consisting of a misanthropic, grief-stricken father and a hired girl. His voice sounded toneless and more tired than ever as he spoke of his childhood.

"Lonely?" queried Sheila.

"Perhaps."

"Neglected and—frightened?"

"What do you mean?"

The girl leaned over the bed and looked straight into the eyes that seemed to be daring her to find the way into his darkness and at the same time barring fast the door against her coming. She smiled gently. "Tell me—can you remember when you first began to fear sleep?"

There was no denial, no protest. Peter sighed as a little worn-out boy might have sighed with the irksome concealment of some forbidden act. "I don't know," he said at last. "I can't think back to a time when I wasn't afraid—afraid of the dropping out, into the dark. God!" He turned his head away, and for the first time in two weary, wakeful nights Sheila saw him close his eyes.

Off duty, instead of going to breakfast and bed, Sheila O'Leary went to the office of the superintendent of nurses. In her usual fashion she came straight to her point. "Put Saunders back on Number Three and give me a couple of days off. Please, Miss Max."

Her abruptness shook the almost unshakable calm of Miss Maxwell. She gazed at the girl in frank amazement. "May I ask why?" There was a kindly irony in the question.

"Sounds queer, I know, but I've simply got to go. Lots depends on it, and no time now to explain. Want to catch that eight-thirty-five; Flanders is holding the bus. Tell you when I get back—please, Miss Max?" And taking consent for granted, Sheila started for the door.

There was an odd look on the face of the superintendent as she watched her go—a look of amused, loving pride. She might hide it from their little world, but she could not deny it to herself, that of all the girls she had helped to train, none had come so close to her heart as this girl with her wonderful insight, her honesty, her plain speaking, and her heart of gold. A hundred times she had defied the rules of the sanitarium, had swept the superintendent's dignity to the four winds. And she would continue to do so, and they would continue to overlook it. Such petty offenses are forgiven the Leeries the world over. And now, watching the gray, alive figure climbing into the omnibus, Miss Maxwell had no mind to resent her breach of discipline. She knew the girl had asked nothing for herself; she had gone to do something for somebody who needed it, and she would report for duty again when that was accomplished.

And two days later, accordingly, she came, a luminous, ecstatic figure that flew into the office with arms outstretched to swing the superintendent almost off her feet in joyful triumph. "It *was* just what I thought! Found the girl—only she is an old woman now—got the whole miserable story from her, and—and—I think—I think—Good heart alive! I think I can pull him out of the beastly old hole!"

"Meaning—? Remember, my dear, I haven't the grain of an idea why you went, or where you went, or what the miserable story is about. Please shine your lantern this way and light up my intelligence." Miss Maxwell was beaming.

Sheila O'Leary laughed. "I began by jumping at conclusions—same as I always do—jumped at 'phobia in Number Three. Almost came and asked to be put on the case after you told me. But he isn't Number Three any more—he's a little boy named Peter—a little boy, almost a baby, frightened night after night for years and years into lying still in the dark under the eaves in a little attic room, deliberately frightened by a hired girl who wanted to be free to go off gadding with her young man. I got the place and her name from Peter—coaxed it out of him—and I made her tell me the story. The father paid her extra wages to stay at night so the little boy wouldn't be lonely and miss his mother too much, and she didn't want him to find out she had gone. So she'd put Peter to bed and tell him that if he stirred or cried out the walls would close in on him—or the floor would swallow him up—or the ghosts would come out of the corners and eat him up or carry him off. Can't you see him there, a little quivering heap of a boy, awake in the dark, afraid to move? Can't you feel how he would lie and listen to all the sounds about him—the squealing mice, the creaking rafters, the wind moaning in the eaves—too terrified to go to sleep? And when he did sleep—worn out—can't you imagine what his dreams would be like? Oh, women like that—women who could frighten little sensitive children—ought to be burned as they burned the witches!" The girl's eyes blazed and she shook a pair of clenched fists into the air. "And can you see the rest of it? How the fear grew and grew even as the memory of the tales faded, grew into a nameless, unexplainable fear of sleep? And because he was a boy he hid it; and because he was a man he fought it; but the thing nailed him at last. He fought sleep until he lost the habit of sleep. He couldn't get along without it, and here he is!"

"Well, what are you going to do?" The superintendent eyed her narrowly; her cheeks were as flushed as the girl's.

A little enigmatical smile curved up the corners of the usually demure mouth. "Going to play Leerie—going to play it harder than I ever did in my life before."

And that night as Peter turned his head wearily toward the door to greet the kindly, cumbersome Saunders, he found, to his surprise, the owner of the shining eyes come back. He felt so ridiculously glad about it that he couldn't even trust himself to tell her so. Instead he repeated foolishly the same old thing, "Why, it's—it's Leerie!"

When everything was ready for the night, Sheila turned the night-light out and lowered the curtain until it was quite dark. Then she drew her chair close to the bed and slipped her hand into the lean, clenched one on the coverlid. "Don't think of me as a girl—a nurse—a person—at all, to-night," she said, softly. "I'm just a piece of Stevenson's poem come to life—a lamplighter for a little boy going to sleep all alone in a farm-house attic. It's very dark. You can hear the mice squeal and the rafters creak, if you listen, and the window's so small the stars can't creep in. In the daytime the attic doesn't seem far away or very strange, but at night it's miles—

miles away from the rest of the house, and it's full of things that may happen. That's why I'm here with my lamp."

Sheila stopped a moment. She could hear the man's breath coming quick, with a catch in it—a child breathes that way when it is fighting down a cry or a sob. Then she went on: "Of course it's a magical lamp I carry, and with the first sputter and spark it lights up and turns the attic inside out—and there we are, the little boy and I, hand in hand, running straight for the brook back of the house. The lamp burns as bright as the sun now, so it seems like day—a spring day. It isn't the mice squealing at all that you hear, but the birds singing and the brook running. There are cowslips down by the brook, and 'Jacks.' Here by the big stone is a chance to build a bully good dam and sailboats made out of the shingles blown off from the barn roof. Want to stop and build it now?"

"All right." There was almost a suppressed laugh in the voice; it certainly sounded glad. And the hand on the coverlid was as relaxed as that of a child being led somewhere it wants to go.

Sheila smiled happily in the dark: "You must get stones, then—lots and lots of them—and we'll pile them together. There's one stone—and two stones—and three stones. Another stone here—another here—another here—a big one there where the current runs swiftest, and little stones for the chinks."

According to Sheila O'Leary's best reckoning the dam was only half built when the little boy fell fast asleep over his work. And when the gray of the morning stole down the corridors of the Surgical, No. 3 was sleeping, with one arm thrown over his head as little boys sleep, and the other holding fast to the nurse on night duty.

But it takes a long while to break down an old habit and build up a new one, as it takes a long while to build a dam. No less than tons of stones must have gone to the building of Peter's before the time came when he could drop asleep alone and unguided. In all that time neither he nor the girl ever spoke of what lay between the putting out of the night lamp and the waking fresh and rested to a welcomed day.

With sleep came speedy recovery, and Peter was the most popular convalescent in the Surgical. His laugh had suddenly grown contagious, his humor irresistible, his outlook on life so optimistically bubbling that less cheery patients turned their wheel-chairs to No. 3 for revitalizing. The chief came up with Doctor Dempsy from town, and both went away wearing the look of men who have seen miracles. Life in its fullness had come to Peter, the life he had dreamed of, as a lost crosser of the desert dreams of water. Efficient work was to be his again, and companionship, and—yes, for the first time he hoped for the third and best of life's ingredients—he hoped for love.

And then, just as everything looked best and brightest, he was told that he no longer needed a night nurse. Sheila O'Leary was put on the case of an old lady with chronic dyspepsia. She told him herself, as she went off duty in the Surgical for the last time.

"You've had the best sleep of all." She smiled at his efforts to pull himself awake. "I'll drop in when I'm passing, to see how you're getting on, but otherwise this is good-by and good luck." She held out her hand.

"Why—but—Hang it all! I can't get along without a night nurse. And if I don't need one, why can't you take Miss Tyler's place in the day?"

"Orders." Sheila announced it as an unshakable fact.

"I'll see Miss Maxwell."

"No use. She wouldn't listen."

"Guess if I'm paying for it I can have—"

Sheila O'Leary's chin squared and her body stiffened. "There are some things no one can pay for, Mr. Brooks."

Peter colored crimson. He reached quickly for the hand Sheila had pulled away. "What an ungrateful cur you must think I am! And I've never said a word—never thanked you."

"There was nothing to thank for. I was only undoing what another woman had done long ago. That's one of the glad things about nursing; we so often have a chance at just that sort of thing—the chance to make up for some of the blind mistakes in life. Good-by. I'm late now."

"But—but—" Peter held frantically to the hand. "'Pon my soul, I can't let you go until—until—" He broke off, crimsoning again. "Promise a time when you will come back—just a minute I can count on and look forward to. Please!"

"All right—I'll be back at four—just for a minute."

It happened, however, that Miss Jacobs—pink-cheeked, auburn-haired, green-eyed little Miss Jacobs, the first nurse on Peter's case, blew into No. 3 a few minutes before four. She had developed the habit of blowing in at least once in the day and telling Peter how perfectly splendid it was to see him getting along so well. But as he did not happen to look quite so well this time, she condoled and wormed the reason out of Peter.

"Leerie off duty! Don't you think it's rather remarkable they let her stay so long? Of course the management, as a rule, doesn't let her have cases of—of this kind. A girl who's been sent away on account of—of—questionable conduct isn't exactly safe to trust. Don't you think so? And the San can't afford to risk its reputation." For an instant the green eyes shimmered and glistened balefully, while she tossed her auburn curls coyly at Peter. "It's really too bad, for she's a wonderful surgical nurse. All the best surgeons want her on their cases. That's why they put her on with you; that's really why they let her come back at all."

A look in Peter's eyes stopped her and made her look back over her shoulder. Sheila O'Leary stood in the open doorway. For an instant the perpetual assurance of Miss Jacobs was shaken, but only for an instant. She smiled tolerantly. "Hello, Leerie! I've been telling Mr. Brooks what a wonderful surgical nurse you are."

The gray eyes of the girl in the doorway looked steadily into the green eyes of the girl by the bed. "Thank you, Coppy, I heard you." And she stepped aside to let the other pass out.

"Well?" she asked when the two were alone.

"Well!" answered Peter, emphatically. "Everything is very, very well. Do you know," and he smiled up at her like a happy small boy—"do you know that all the while you were building that dam I was building something else?"

"Were you?"

"I was building my life over again—building it fresh, with the fear gone and everything sound and strong and fine. And into the chinks where all the miserable empty places had been—the places where loneliness and heartache eternally leaked through—I was fitting love, the love I never dared dream of."

"Yes?"

The girl's lips looked strangely hard—almost bitter, Peter thought; and this time he reached out both arms to her.

"Hang it all! It's tough on a man who's never dared dream of love to have it take him, bandaged and tied to his bed. Leerie—Leerie! You wouldn't have the heart to blow out the lamp now, would you?"

The lips softened, she gave a sad little shake of her head. "No, but you've got to keep it burning yourself. You're a man; you can do it. Sorry—can't help it. And please don't say anything more. Don't spoil it all, and make me say things I wish I hadn't and send you off to pay your bill and leave the

San to-night." She smiled wistfully. "Dear, grown-up boy! Don't you know that it's the customary thing for a man to think he's fallen in love with his nurse when he's convalescing? Just get well and forget it—as all the others do." She turned toward the door.

"I'm not going to pay my bill to-night, and I'm not going to forget it. I guess all those chinks haven't been filled up yet. I'm going to stay until they are. Good plan, don't you think?" And Peter Brooks smiled like a man who had never been given up—nor ever intended giving up, now that life had given him back the things for which he had a right to fight.

Chapter II

OLD KING COLE

HENNESSY was feeding the swans. Sheila O'Leary leaned over the sill of the diminutive rustic rest-house and watched him with a tired contentment. She had just come off a neurasthenic case—a week of twenty-four-hour duty—and she wanted to stretch her cramped sensibilities in the quiet peace of the little house and invite her soul with a glimpse of Hennessy and the swans.

All about her the grounds of the sanitarium were astir with its customary crowd of early-summer-afternoon patients. How those first warm days called the sick folks out-of-doors and held them there until the last beam of sunshine had disappeared behind the foremost hill! The tennis-courts were full; the golf-links were dotted about with spots of color like a cubist picture; pairs of probationers, arm in arm, were strolling about, enjoying a comparative leisure; old Madam Courot was at her customary place under the juniper, watching the sun go down. Three years! Nothing seemed changed in all that time but the patients—and not all of these, as Madame Courot silently testified. The pines shook themselves above the rest-house in the same lazy, vagabond fashion, the sun purpled the far hills and spun the same yellow haze over the links, the wind brought its habitual afternoon accompaniment of cow-bells from the sanitarium farm, and Hennessy threw the last crumb of bread to Brian Boru, the gray swan, as he had done for the fifteen years Sheila could remember.

She folded her arms across the sill and rested her chin on them. How good it was to be back at the old San, to settle down to its kindly, comfortable ways and the peace of its setting after the feverish restlessness of city hospitals! She remembered what Kipling had said, that the hill people who came down to the plains were always hungering to get back to the hills again. That was the way she had felt about it—always a hunger to come back. For months and months she had thought that she might forever have to stay in those hospitals, have to make up her mind to the eternal plains—and then had come her reprieve—she had been called back to the San and the work she loved best.

Had the place been any other than the sanitarium, and the person any other than Sheila O'Leary, this would never have happened. For she had left under a cloud, and in similar cases a cloud, once gathered, grows until it envelops, suffocates, and finally annihilates the person. As a graduate nurse she would have ceased to exist. But in spite of the most blighting circumstances, those who counted most believed in her and trusted her. They had only waited for time to forget and tongues to stop wagging, and then they had called her back. Perhaps the strangest thing about it was that Sheila did not look like a person who could have had even the smallest, fleeciest of clouds brushing her most distant horizon. In fact, so vital, warm, and glowing was her personality, so radiant her nature, that she seemed instead a permanent dispeller of clouds.

From across the pond Hennessy watched her with adoring eyes as he gave his habitual, final bang to the bread-platter and the hitch to his corduroys preparatory to leaving. To his way of thinking, there was no nurse enrolled on the books of the old San who could compare with her. In the beginning he had prophesied great things of her to Flanders, the bus-driver. "Ye mind what I'm tellin' ye," he had said. "Afore she's finished her trainin' she'll have more lads a-dandtherin' round her than if she'd been the King of Ireland's only daughter. Ye can take my word for it, when she leaves here, 'twill be a grand home of her own she'll be goin' to an' no dirty hospital."

That had been three years ago, and Hennessy sighed now over the utter futility of his words. "Sure, who could have been seein' that one o' the lads would have turned blackguard? Hennessy knows. Just give the lass time for that hurt to heal, an' she'll be winnin' a home of her own, after all." This he muttered to himself as he took the path leading toward the rest-house.

Sheila saw him coming, his lips shirred to the closeness of some emotional strain. "Hello, Hennessy! What's troubling?" she called down the path.

"Faith, it's Mr. Peter Brooks that's troublin'. 'Tis a week, now, that ye've been off that case—an' he's near cured. Another week now—"

"In another week he'll be going back to his work—and I'll be very glad."

Hennessy eyed the girl narrowly. "Will ye, then? Why did ye cure him up so fast for, Miss Leerie? Why didn't ye give the poor man a chance?"

No one but Hennessy would have had sufficient temerity for such a question, but had any one dared to ask it, upon their heads would have fallen the combined anger and bitterness of Sheila's tongue. For having had occasion once for bitterness, it was not over-hard to waken it when men served as topics. But at Hennessy she smiled tolerantly. "Didn't I give him a chance to get well? That was all he needed or wanted. And, now he's well, he'll go about his business."

"Faith," and Hennessy closed a suggestive eye, "that depends on what he takes to be his business. In my young days the choosin' an' courtin' of a wife was the big part of a man's business. Now if he comes round askin' my opinion—"

"Tell him, Hennessy"—and Sheila fixed him firmly with a glance—"that the sanitarium does not encourage its cured patients to hang about bothering its nurses. It is apt to make trouble for the nurses. Understand?"

Again Hennessy closed one eye; then he laughed. "When ye talk of devils ye're sure to smell brimstone. There comes Mr. Brooks now, an' he has his head back like a dog trailin' the wind."

The girl turned and followed Hennessy's jerking thumb with her eyes. Across the pine grove, coming toward them, was a young man above medium height, square-shouldered and erect. There was nothing startlingly handsome nor remarkable about his appearance; he was just nice, strong, clean-looking. He waved to the two by the rest-house.

"And do ye mind his looks when he came!" Hennessy's tone denoted wonder and admiration.

"A human wreck—haunted at that." There was a good deal more than mere professional interest in Sheila's tone; there was pride and something else. It was past Hennessy's perceptive powers to define what, but he noticed it, nevertheless, and looked sharply up at the girl.

"For the love o' Mike, Miss Leerie! Why can't ye stop ticketin' each man as a case an' begin thinkin' about them human-like? Ye might begin practisin' wi' Mr. Brooks."

The line of Sheila's lips became fixed; the chin that could look so demure, the eyes that could look so soft and gentle, both backed up the lips in an expression of inscrutable hardness.

"In the name of your patron saint, Hennessy, what have you said to Miss Leerie to turn her into that sphinx again?" The voice of Peter Brooks was as nice as his appearance.

Hennessy looked foolish. "I was tellin' her, then," he moistened his lips to allow a safer emigration of words—"I was tellin' her—that the gray swan had the rheumatism in his left leg, an' I was askin' her, did she think Doctor Willum would prescribe a thermo bath for him. I'd best be askin' him meself, maybe," and with a sudden pull at his forelock Hennessy backed away down the path.

Peter Brooks watched him depart with an admiration equal to that with which Hennessy had welcomed him. "That man has a wonderful insight into human nature. Now I was just wishing I could have you all alone for about—"

Sheila interrupted him. "I hope you weren't counting on too many minutes. I can see Miss Maxwell coming down the San steps, and I have a substantial feeling that she's looking for me to put me on another case."

"Couldn't we escape? Couldn't we skip round by the farm to the garage and get my car? You look fagged out. A couple of hours' ride would do wonders for you, and—Good Lord! The San can run that long without your services. What do you say? Shall we beat it?"

With a telltale, pent-up eagerness he noticed the girl's indecision and flung himself with all his persuasive powers to turn the balance in his favor. "Do come. You can work better and harder for a little time off now and then. All the other nurses take it. Why under the heavens can't a man ever persuade you to have a little pleasure?" Something in Sheila's face stopped him and prompted the one argument that could have persuaded her. "If you'll only come, Leerie, I'll promise to keep dumb—absolutely dumb. I'll promise not to spoil the ride for you."

Sheila flung him a radiant smile; it almost unbalanced him and murdered his resolve. "Then I'll come. You're the first man I ever knew who could keep his word—that way. Hurry! we'll have to run for it." And taking the lead, she ducked through the little door of the rest-house and ran, straight as the crow flies, to the hiding shelter of the farm.

But her premonition was correct. When she returned two hours later in the cool of a summer's twilight, with eyes that sparkled like iridescent pools and lips that smiled generously her gratitude to the man who could keep his word, she found the superintendent of nurses watching from the San steps for their car.

"All right, Miss Maxwell," she nodded in response to the question that was plainly stamped on the superintendent's face. "We've had supper—don't even have to change my uniform." Then to Peter, "Thank you."

The words were meager enough, but Peter Brooks had already received his compensation in the girl's glowing face. "It's 'off again, on again, gone again,' in your profession, too. Well, here's looking forward to the next escape." His laugh rang with health and good spirits.

Sheila stopped on her way up the steps, turned and looked back at him. The wonder of his recovery often surprised even herself. It seemed incredible that this pulsing, vitalized portion of humanity could have once been a veritable husk, hounded by a haunting fear into a state of hopelessness and loathing of existence. Life certainly tingled in Peter now, and every time Sheila felt it, man or no man, she could not help rejoice with all her heart at the thing she had helped to do.

Peter's smile met hers half-way in the dusk. "It may be another week before I see you again. In case—I'd like to tell you that I'm staying on indefinitely. The chief has pushed me out of my Sunday section and has sent me a lot of special articles to do up here. He thinks I had better not come back until I'm all fit."

"You're perfectly fit now." There was a brutal frankness in the girl's words.

Peter had grown used to these moments. They no longer troubled or hurt him. He had begun to understand. "Maybe I am; I feel so, but you can never tell. Then there's always the danger of one's heart going back on one. That's why I've decided to stay on and coddle mine. Rather good plan?"

Sheila O'Leary vouchsafed no answer. She disappeared through the entrance of the sanitarium, leaving Peter Brooks still smiling. Neither his expression nor position had changed a few seconds later when Miss Jacobs touched him on the arm.

"Oh, Mr. Brooks! Were you the guilty party—running away with Leerie? For the last two hours we've been combing the San grounds for her." The green eyes of the flirtatious nurse gleamed peculiarly catlike in the dusk. "Of course I don't suppose my opinion counts so very much with you," there was a honeyed, self-deprecatory quality in the girl's tone, "but if I were you, I wouldn't go about so awfully much with Leerie. She's a dear girl—I don't suppose it's really her fault—but she had such a record. And you know it's my creed that girls of that kind can compromise poor men far oftener than men compromise girls. Oh, I do hope you understand what I mean!"

Peter still wore a smile, but it was a different smile. It was as much like the old one as a search-light is like sunshine. He focused it full on Miss Jacobs's face. "I'm a shark at understanding. And don't worry about me. I'm more of a shark in deep water with—with sirens." He chuckled inwardly at the look of blank incomprehension on the nurse's face. "By the way, just what did you want Miss Leary for? Not another accident?"

The girl gave her head a disgusted toss. "Oh, they want her to help an old man die. He came up here a week ago. I saw him then, and he looked ready to burst. Doctor MacByrn said he weighed over three hundred and had a blood pressure of two hundred and ten. They can't bring it down, and his heart is about done for. Leerie always gets those dying cases. Ugh!" The girl shuddered. "Guess they wouldn't put me on any of those sure-dead cases; it's bad enough when you happen on them."

Peter shot her a pitying glance and walked back to his car. He was just climbing in when the girl's voice chirped back to him. "Just the night for a ride, isn't it? I couldn't think of letting you go all alone and be lonesome. Isn't it lucky I'm off duty till ten!"

"Lucky for the patient!" Peter mumbled under his breath; then aloud: "Sorry, but I'm unlucky. Only enough gasoline to get her back to the garage. Good night." He swung the car free of the curb, leaving little red-headed, green-eyed Miss Jacobs in the process of gathering up her skirts and mounting into thin air.

Meanwhile Sheila had followed the superintendent to her office. "It's a case of cerebral hemorrhages. The man is no fool; he knows his condition, and he's been getting increasingly hard to take care of every minute since he found out. Maybe you've heard of him. He's Brandle, the coal magnate. Quite alone in the world; no children, and his wife died some few years ago. He's very peculiar, and no one seems to know what to say to him or do for him. I'm a little afraid—" and the superintendent paused to consider her words before committing herself. "I think perhaps there have been too many offers of prayers and scriptural readings for his taste."

"Probably he'd prefer the last *Town Topics* or the latest detective story." Sheila shook her head violently. "Why can't a man be allowed to die the way he chooses—instead of your way, or my way, or the Reverend Mr. Grumble's way?"

"Miss Barry is on the case now, and I'm afraid he's shocked her into—"

"Perpetual devotion." Sheila grinned sympathetically as she completed the sentence. They had called her Prayer-Book Barry her probation year because of her unswerving religious point of view, and her years of training had only served to increase it. The picture of anything as sensitively pious as Prayer-Book Barry helping a coal magnate to depart this temporal world in his own chosen fashion was too much for Sheila's sense of the grotesque. She threw back her head and laughed. Peal after peal rang out and over the transom of the superintendent's office just as Miss Jacobs passed.

It took no great powers of penetration to identify the laugh; a look of satisfaction crept into the green eyes. "Quite dramatic and brutally unfeeling I call it," she murmured. "But it will make an entertaining story to tell Mr. Brooks. He thinks Leerie is such a little tinseled saint."

Ten minutes later Sheila O'Leary followed Miss Maxwell into the large tower room of the sanitarium to relieve Miss Barry from duty. As she took her first look from the doorway she almost forgot herself and laughed again. The room might have been a scene set for a farce or a comic opera.

Propped up in bed, with multitudinous pillows about him, was a very mammoth of a man in heliotrope-silk pajamas. His face was as round and full and bucolic as a poster advertising some specific brew of beer. Surmounting the face was a sparse fringe of white hair standing erect, while an isolated lock mounted guard over a receding forehead. It was evident that the natural expression of the face was good-natured, indulgent, easygoing, but at the moment of Sheila's entrance it was contorted into something that might have served for a cartoon of a choleric full moon. The eyes were rolling frantically in every direction but that from which the presumable infliction came, for seated at the bedside, with a booklet of evening prayer open on her lap, was Miss Barry, reading aloud in a sweet, gentle voice.

Miss Barry did not stop until she had finished her paragraph. The cessation of her voice brought the roving eyes to a standstill; then they flew straight to Miss Maxwell in abject appeal. "Take it away, ma'am. Don't hurt it—but take it away!" The articulation was thick, but it did not mask the wail in the voice, and a gigantic thumb jerked indicatively toward the patient, asserting figure of Miss Barry.

"All right, Mr. Brandle." Miss Maxwell's tone showed neither conciliation nor pity; it was plainly matter-of-fact. "As it happens, I've brought you a new nurse. Suppose you try Miss O'Leary for the next day or two."

The wail broke out afresh: "How can I tell if I can stand her? They all look alike—all of 'em. You're the fourth, ain't you?" He turned to the nurse at his bedside for corroboration.

"Then I'm the fifth," announced Sheila, "and there's luck in odd numbers."

"Five's my number." The mammoth man looked a fraction less distracted as he stated this important fact. "Born fifth day of the fifth month, struck it rich when I was twenty-five, married in 'seventy-five, formed the American Coal Trust December fifth, eighteen ninety-five. How's that for a number?"

"And I'm twenty-five, and this is June fifth." Sheila smiled.

"Say, honest?" A glimmer of cheerfulness filtered through. The man beckoned the superintendent of nurses closer and whispered in a perfectly audible voice: "Can't you take it away now? I'd like to ask the other some questions before you leave her for keeps."

Miss Maxwell nodded a dismissal to the nurse who had been, and called Sheila to the bedside. "Look her over well, Mr. Brandle. Miss O'Leary isn't a bit sensitive."

"O'Leary? That's not a bad name. Had a shaft boss up at my first anthracite-mine by that name—got on with him first-class. Say"—this direct to Sheila—"can you pray?"

"Not unless I have to."

"Not a bad answer. Now what—er—form of—literatoore do you prefer?"

"Things with pep—punch—go!"

"Say, shake." The mammoth man smiled as he held out a giant fist. Sheila had the feeling she was shaking hands with some prehistoric animal. It was almost repellent, and she had to summon all her sympathy and control to be able to return the shake with any degree of cordiality.

"All right, ma'am. You can leave us now to thrash it out man to man. You'd better get back to managing your little white angels," and he swept a dismissing hand toward Miss Maxwell and the door.

Oddly enough, there was nothing rude nor affronting in the man's words. There was too much of underlying good nature to permit it. With the closing of the door behind the superintendent he turned to Sheila. "Now, boss, we might as well understand each other—it'll save strikes or hurt feelings. Eh?"

Sheila nodded.

"All right. I'm dying, and I know it. May burst like a paper bag or go up like a penny balloon any minute. Now praying won't keep me from bursting a second sooner, or send me up a foot higher, so cut it out."

Again Sheila nodded.

"That isn't all. Had two nurses who agreed, kept their word, but they hadn't the nerve to keep the parson from praying, and when he was off duty they just sat—twiddled their thumbs and waited for me to quit. Couldn't stand that—got on my nerves something fearful."

"Wanted to murder them, didn't you?" Sheila laughed. "Well, Mr. Brandle, suppose we begin with supper and the baseball news. After that we'll hunt up a thriller—biggest thriller they've got in the book-store."

"You're boss," was the answer, but a look of relief—almost of contentment—spread over the rubicund face.

As Sheila was leaving for the supper-tray she paused. "How would you like company for supper?"

"Company? Good Lord, not the parson!"

"No, me. If you are willing to sign for two, I could bring my supper up with yours."

"And not eat alone! By Jehoshaphat! Give me that slip quick."

They had not only a good supper, they had a noisy one. The coal magnate roared over Sheila's descriptions of some of the bath treatments and their victims. In the midst of one particularly noisy explosion he suddenly stopped and looked accusingly at her. "Why don't you stop me? Don't you know doctor's orders? Had 'em dinged into my head until I could say 'em backwards: no exertion, no excitement, avoid all undue movement, keep quiet. Darn it all! As if I won't have to keep quiet long enough! Well—why don't you repeat those fool orders and keep me quiet?"

Sheila looked at him with a pair of steady gray eyes. "Do you know, Mr. Brandle, it isn't a half-bad way to go out of this world—to go laughing."

The mammoth man beamed. He looked for all the world like the full moon suddenly grown beatific. "And I'd just about made up my mind that I'd never find a blamed soul who would feel that way about it. Shake again, boss."

After the baseball news and a fair start in the thriller, he indulged further in past grievances. "Hadn't any more'n settled it for sure I was done for than the parson came and the nurse took to looking mournful. Lord Almighty! ain't it bad enough to be carted off in a hearse once without folks putting you in beforehand? That's not my notion of dying. I lived pleasant and cheerful, and by the Lord Harry, I don't see why I can't die that way! And look-a-here, boss, I don't want any of that repenting stuff. I don't need no puling parson to tell me I'm a sinner. Any idiot couldn't look at me without guessing that much. Say!" He leaned forward with sudden earnestness. "Take a good look at me yourself. See any halo or angel trappings about me?"

Sheila laughed. "I'm afraid not. What you really ought to have—what I miss about you—is the pipe, and the bowl, and the fiddlers three."

"What do you mean by that?"

"Don't you remember? It's an old nursery rhyme; probably you heard it hundreds of times when you were a little boy:

> "Old King Cole was a merry old soul
> And a merry old soul was he.
> He called for his pipe and he called for his bowl,
> And he called for his fiddlers three."

The coal magnate threw back his head on the pillows and laughed long and loud. He laughed until he grew purple and gasped for breath, and he laughed while he choked, and Sheila flew about for stimulants. For a few breathless moments Sheila thought she had whipped up the hearse—to use the mammoth man's own metaphor—but after a panting half-hour the heart subsided and the breath came easier.

"You nearly did for me that time, boss. But it fits; Jehoshaphat, it fits me like a B. V. D.! The only difference you might put down to simplified spelling. Eh?" And he cautiously chuckled at his joke.

While Sheila was making ready for the night he chuckled and lapsed into florid, heliotrope studies by turns. "It's straight, what I told you about being a sinner," he gave verbal expression to his thoughts at last. "That's why I don't leave a cent to charity—not a cent. Ain't going to have any peaked-faced, oily-tongued jackasses saying over my coffin that I tried to buy my entrance ticket into the Lord Almighty's kingdom. No, sirree! I know I've lived high, eaten well, and drunk some. I've made the best of every good bargain that came within eyeshot. I treated my own handsome—and I let the rest of the world go hang. Went to church Easter Sunday every year and put a bill in the plate; you can figure for yourself about how much I've given to charity. Never had any time to think of it, anyway—probably wouldn't have given if I had. Always thought Mother'd live longer'n me and she'd take care of that end of it. But she didn't."

For a moment Sheila thought the man was going to cry; his lower lip quivered like a baby's, and his eyes grew red and watery. There was no denying it, the man was a caricature; even his grief was ludicrous. He wiped his eyes with the back of his heliotrope sleeve and finished what he had to say. "Don't it beat all how the pious vultures croak over you the minute you're done for—reminding you you can't take your money away with you? Didn't the parson—first time he came—sit in that chair and open up and begin about the rich man's squeezing through a needle's eye and a lot about putting away temporal stuff? I don't aim to do any squeezing into heaven, I can tell you. And I fixed him all right. Ha, ha! I told him as long as the money wouldn't do me and Mother any more good I'd settle it so's it couldn't benefit any one else. And that's exactly what I've done. Left it all for a monument for us, fancy marble, carved statues, and the whole outfit. It'll beat that toadstool-looking tomb of that prince somewhere in Asia all hollow. Ha, ha!"

He leaned back to enjoy to the full this humorous legacy to himself, but the expression of Sheila's face checked it. "Say, boss, you don't like what I've done, do you? Run it out and dump it; I can stand for straight talk from you."

Sheila felt repelled even more than she had at first. To have a man at the point of death throw his money into a heap of marble just to keep it from doing good to any one seemed horrible. And yet the man spoke so consistently for himself. He had lived in the flesh and for the flesh all his days; it was not strange that there was no spirit to interpret now for him or to give him the courage to be generous in the face of what the world would think.

"It's yours to spend as you like—only—I hate monuments. Rather have the plain green grass over me. And don't you think it's queer yourself that a man who had the grit to make himself and a pile of money hasn't the grit to leave it invested after he goes, instead of burying it? Supposing you can't live and use it yourself! That's no reason for not letting your money live after you. I'd want to keep my money alive."

"Alive? Say, what do you mean?"

"Just what I say—alive. Charity isn't the only way to dispose of it. Leave it to science to discover something new with; give it to the laboratories to study up typhoid or cancer. Ever think how little we know about them?"

"Why should I? I don't owe anything to science."

"Yes, you do. What developed the need of coal—what gave you the facilities for removing it from your mines? Don't tell me you or anybody else doesn't owe something to science."

"Bosh!" And the argument ended there.

The old man had a good night. He dozed as peacefully as if he had not required propping up and occasional hypodermics to keep his lungs and heart going properly, and when the house doctor made his early rounds this sad and shocking spectacle met his eye: the dying coal magnate, arrayed in a fresh and more vivid suit of heliotrope pajamas, smoking a brierwood and keeping a violent emotional pace with the hero in the thrillingest part of the thriller. Even Sheila's cheeks were tinged with excitement.

"Miss O'Leary!" All the outraged sensibilities of an orthodox, conscientious young house physician were plainly manifested in those two words.

Out shot the brierwood like a projectile, and a giant finger wagged at the intruder. "Look-a-here, young man, the boss and I are running this—er—quitting game to suit ourselves, and we don't need no suggestions from the walking delegate, or the board of directors, or the gang. See? Now if you can't say something pleasant and cheerful, get out!"

"Good morning!" It was the best compromise the house physician could make. But ten minutes after his speedy exit Doctor Greer, the specialist, and Miss Maxwell were on the threshold, both looking unmistakably troubled.

The coal magnate winked at Sheila. "Here comes the peace delegates—or maybe it's from the labor union. Well, sir?" This was shot straight at the doctor.

"Mr. Brandle, you're mad. I refuse to take any responsibility."

"Don't have to. That's what's been the matter—too much responsibility. It got on my nerves. Now we want to be as—as noisy and as happy as we can, the boss and me. And if we can't do it in this little old medicated brick-pile of yours, why, we'll move. See? Or I'll buy it with a few tons of my coal and give it to the boss to run."

"When it's yours." The specialist was finding it hard to keep his temper. The man had worn him out in the week he had been at the sanitarium. It had been harder to manage him than a spoiled child or a lunatic. He had had to humor him, cajole him, entreat him, in a way that galled his professional dignity, and now to have the man deliberately and publicly kill himself in this fashion was almost beyond endurance. He tried hard to make his voice sound agreeable as well as determined when he launched his ultimatum. "But in the mean time Miss O'Leary will have to be removed from the case."

"No, you don't!" With a sweep of the giant hand the bedclothes were jerked from their roots, and a pair of heliotrope legs projected floorward. It took the strength of all the three present to hold him back and replace the covering. The magnate sputtered and fumed. "First nurse you put on here after the boss goes—I'll die on her hands in ten minutes just to get even with you. That's what I'll do. And what's more—I'll come back to haunt the both of you. Take away my boss—just after we get things going pleasantly. Spoil a poor man's prospects of dying cheerful! Haven't you any heart, man? And you, ma'am?" this to the superintendent of nurses. "By the Lord Harry! you're a woman—you ought to have a little sympathy!" The aggressiveness died out of the voice, and it took on the old wail Sheila had first heard.

"But you forget my professional responsibility in the matter—my principles as an honorable member of my profession. I cannot allow a patient of mine wilfully to endanger his life—even shorten it. You must understand that, Mr. Brandle."

A look of amused toleration spread over the rubicund face. "Bless your heart, sonny, you're not allowing me to shorten it one minute. The boss and I are prolonging it first-rate. Shouldn't wonder if it would get to be so pleasant having her around I'd be working over union hours and forgetting to quit at all. I'm old enough to be your granddaddy, so take a bit of advice from me. When you can't cure a patient, let 'em die their own way. Now run along, sonny. Good morning, ma'am." And then to Sheila: "Get back to that locked door, the three bullet-holes, and the blood patch on the floor. I've got to know what's on the other side before I touch one mouthful of that finnan haddie you promised me for breakfast."

After that Old King Cole had his way. The doctors visited him as a matter of form, and Sheila improvised a chart, for he would not stand for having temperatures taken or pulses counted. "Cut it out, boss, cut it all out. We're just going to have a good time, you and me." And he smiled seraphically as he drummed on the spread:

> "Old King Cole—diddy-dum-diddy-dum,
> Was a merry old soul—diddy-dum-diddy-dum."

On the second day Sheila introduced Peter Brooks into the "Keeping-On-Going Syndicate," as the mammoth man termed their temporary partnership. Sheila had to take some hours off duty, and as the coal magnate absolutely refused to let another nurse cross his threshold, Peter seemed to be the only practical solution. She knew the two men would get on admirably. Peter could be counted on to understand and meet any emergency that might arise, while Old King Cole would be kept content. And Sheila was right.

"Say, we hit it off first-rate—ran together as smooth as a parcel o' greased tubs," the magnate confided to Sheila when she returned. "He told me a whole lot about you—what you did for him—and the nickname they'd given you—'Leerie.' I like that, but I like my name for you better. Eh, boss?"

Once admitted, Peter often availed himself of his membership in the syndicate. He made a third at their games, turned an attentive ear to the thriller or added his bit to the enlightenment of the conversation. And there wasn't a topic from war to feminine-dress reform that they did not attack and thrash out among them with all the keenness and thoroughness of three alive and original minds.

"Puts me thinking of the days when I was switch boss at the Cassie Maguire Mine. Nothing but a shaver then, working up; nothing to do in the God-forsaken hole, after work, but talk. We just about settled the affairs of the world and gave the Lord Almighty advice into the bargain." The mammoth man laughed a mammoth laugh. "And when we'd talked ourselves inside out we'd have some fiddling—always a fiddle among some of the boys. Never hear one of those old tunes that it don't take me back to the Cassie Maguire and the way a fiddle would play the heart back into a lonely, homesick shaver." He turned with a suspicious sniff to Sheila. "Come, boss, the chessboard. Peter'n'me are going to have another Verdun set-to. Only this time he's German. See? And if you don't mind, you might fill up our pipes and bring us our four-forty bowl."

At one time of the day only did the merriment flag—that was at dusk. "Don't like it—never did like it," he confessed. "Something about it that gets onto my chest and turns me gloomy. Don't suppose you ever smelled the choke-damp, did you? Well, that's the feeling. Say, boss, wouldn't be a bad plan to shine up that old safety of yours and give us more light in the old pit. Mother quit about this time o' day, and it seems like I can't forget it."

The next day the coal magnate took a turn for the worse. The heart specialist and the house doctor glowered ominously at Sheila as they came to make their unwelcome rounds, and Sheila hurried them out of the room as speedily as she could. Then it was that she thought of the fiddlers three. An out-of-town orchestra played biweekly at the sanitarium. They were young men, most of them, still apprentices at their art, and she knew they would be glad enough for extra earnings. They were due that evening, and she would engage the services of three violins for the dusk hour the old man dreaded. She did not accomplish this without a protest from the business office, warnings from the two physicians, and shocked comments from the habitual gossips of the sanitarium. But Sheila held her ground and fought for her way against their combined attacks. "Of course I know he's dying. Don't care if the whole San faints with mortification. I'm going to see he dies the way he wants to—keep it merry till the end."

To the Reverend Mr. Grumble, who requested—nay, demanded—admittance, she turned a deaf ear while she held the door firmly closed behind her. "Can't come in. Sorry, he doesn't want you. If you must say a last prayer to comfort yourself, say it in some other room. It will do Old King Cole just as much good and keep him much happier. Now, please go!"

So it happened that only Peter was present when the musicians arrived. Sheila ushered them in with a flourish. "Old King Cole, your fiddlers three. Now what shall they play?"

Lucky for the indwellers of the sanitarium that the magnate's room was in the tower and therefore little sound escaped. It is improbable if the final ending would ever have been known to any but those present, whose discretion could have been relied upon, but for the fact that Miss Jacobs stood with her ear to the keyhole for fully ten minutes. It was surprising how quickly everybody knew about it after that. It created almost as much scandal as Sheila's own exodus had three years before. Many had the temerity to take the lift to the third floor and pace with attentive ears the corridor that led to the tower. These came back to fan the flame of shocked excitement below. The doctors and Mr. Grumble came to Miss Maxwell to interfere and put an end to this ungodly and unprofessional humoring of one departing soul. But the superintendent of nurses refused. She had put the case in Sheila's hands, and she had absolute faith in her. So all that was left to the busybodies and the scandalmongers was to hear what they could and give free rein to their tongues.

There was, however, one mitigating fact: they could listen, and they could talk, but they could not look beyond the closed door of the tower room. That vivid, appalling picture was mercifully denied them. With a heaping bowl of egg-nog beside him, and his brierwood between his lips, the coal magnate beat time on the bedspread with a fast-failing strength, while he grinned happily at Sheila. Beside him Peter lounged in a wheel-chair, smoking for company, while grouped about the foot of the bed in the attitude of a small celestial choir stood the fiddlers three.

All the good old tunes, reminiscent of younger days of mining-camps and dance-halls, they played as fast as fingers could fly and bows could scrape. "Dan Tucker," "Money Musk," "The Irish Washerwoman," and "Pop Goes the Weasel" sifted in melodic molecules through the keyhole into the curious and receptive ears outside. And after them came "Captain Jinks" and "The Blue Danube," "Yankee Doodle" and "Dixie."

"Some boss!" muttered the magnate, thickly, the brierwood dropping on the floor. "Just one solid streak of anthracite—clear through. Now give us something else—I don't care—you choose it, boss."

So Leerie chose "The Star-spangled Banner" and "Marching Through Georgia," and as dusk crept closer about them, "Suwanee River" and "The Old Kentucky Home."

"Nice, sleepy old tunes," mumbled the coal magnate. "Guess I've napped over-time." He opened one eye and looked at Sheila, half amused, half puzzled. "Say, boss, light up that little old lamp o' yours and take me down; the shaft's growing pretty black."

The fiddlers played a hymn as their own final contribution. Sheila smiled wistfully across the dusk to Peter. She knew it wouldn't matter now, for Old King Cole was passing beyond the reach of hymns, prayers, or benedictions.

"It's over as far as you or I or he are concerned," she whispered, whimsically. "When I come down, by and by, would you very much mind taking me on one of those rides you promised? I want to forget that white-marble monument."

It was not until a week later that Sheila O'Leary met with one of the big surprises of her rather eventful existence. A lawyer came down from New York and asked for her. It seemed that the coal magnate had left her a considerable number of thousands to spend for him and ease her feelings about the monument. The codicil was quaintly worded and stated that inasmuch as "Mother" had gone first, he guessed she would do the next best by him.

Sheila took Peter Brooks into her immediate confidence. "Half of it goes for typhoid research and half for a nurses' home here. We've needed one dreadfully. What staggers me is when did he do it?"

Peter grinned. "When I happened to be on duty. We fixed it up, and I was to keep the secret. He had lots of fun over it—poor old soul!"

"Merry old soul," corrected Sheila.

And when the nurses' home was built Sheila flatly ignored all the suggestions of a memorial tablet with appropriate scriptural verses to grace the cornerstone or hang in the entrance-hall.

"Won't have it—never do in the world! Just going to have his picture over the living-room fireplace."

And there it hangs—a gigantic reproduction of Old King Cole, done by the greatest poster artist of America.

Chapter III

THE CHANGELING

HE arrived in the arms of his mother, the mulatto nurse having in some inexplicable and inconsiderate fashion acquired measles on the ship coming from their small South American republic. Francisco Enrique Manuel Machado y Rodriguez—Pancho, for short—and his mother were allowed to disembark only because of his appalling lack of health and her promise to take harborage in a hospital instead of a hotel.

Having heard of the sanitarium from her sister-in-law's brother's wife's aunt, who had been there herself, and having traveled already over a thousand miles, the additional hundred or so seemed too trivial to bother about. So the señora kept her promise to the officials by buying her ticket thitherward, and Flanders, the bus-driver, arrived just in time to see three porters unload them and their luggage on the small station platform. The señora was weeping bitterly, the powder spattered and smeared all over her pretty, shallow little face; Pancho was clawing and scratching the air, while he shrieked at the top of his lungs—the only part of him that gave any evidence of strength.

Having disposed of the luggage, Flanders hurried back to the assistance of the señora, whereupon the brown atom clawed him instead of the air and fortissimoed his shrieking. Flanders promptly returned him to his mother, backing away to the bus and muttering something about "letting wildcat's cubs be."

"Wil'cat?" repeated the señora through her sobs. "I don't know what ees wil'cat. I theenk eet ees one leetle deevil. Tsa, Panchito! Ciera la boca." And she shook him.

During the drive to the sanitarium Flanders cast periodic glances within. Each time he looked the atom appeared to be shrieking louder, while his mother was shaking harder and longer. By the time they had reached their destination the breath had been shaken quite out of him. He lay back panting in his mother's arms, with only strength enough for a feeble and occasional snarl. His bonnet of lace and cerise-pink ribbon had come untied and had slipped from his head, disclosing a mass of black hair curled by nature and matted by neglect. It gave the last uncanny touch to the brown atom's appearance and caused Hennessy, who was sweeping the crossing, to drop his broom and stare agape at the new arrivals.

"Faith, is it one o' them Brazilian monkeys?" he whispered, pulling Flanders by the sleeve. "I've heard the women are makin' pets o' them, although I never heard they were after fixin' them up wi' lace an' ribbons like that."

"It's a kid." Flanders stated the fact without any degree of positiveness as he rubbed three fingers cautiously down his cheek. He was feeling for scars. "Guess it's a kid all right, but it scratches like a cat, gosh durn it!"

Hennessy, however, shook a positive head. "That's no kid. Can't ye see for yourself it's noways human? Accordin' to the Sunday papers it's all the style for blond dancers an' society belles to be fetchin' one o' them little apes about. They're thinkin' if they hang a bit o' live ugliness furninst, their beauty will look all the more ravishin'."

"Live ugliness," repeated Flanders; then he laughed. "You've struck it, Hennessy."

Meanwhile Francisco Enrique Manuel Machado y Rodriguez—Pancho, for short—and his mother had passed into the hands of the sanitarium porter. He had handed them on to the business office, which in turn had handed them over to the superintendent. The superintendent had shared the pleasure with the house staff, the staff had retired in favor of the baby specialist, and at half past seven o'clock that night neither he nor the superintendent of nurses had been able to coax, argue, command, or threaten a nurse into taking the case.

"I'm afraid you will have to do with an undergraduate and make the best of it." Miss Maxwell acknowledged her helplessness with a faint smile.

But Doctor Fuller shook his head. "Won't do. It means skilled care and watching for days. A nurse without experience would be about as much good as an incubator. Think if you dismissed the four who've refused, you could frighten a fifth into taking it?"

This time the superintendent of nurses shook her head. "Not this case. They all feel about it the same way. Miss Jacobs tells me she didn't take her training to nurse monkeys."

The old doctor chuckled. "Don't know as I blame her; thought it was a new species myself when I first clapped eyes on it. But shucks! I've seen some of our North American babies look like Lincoln Imps when they were down with marasmus. Give me a few weeks and a good nurse and his own mother wouldn't recognize—" He interrupted himself with a pounding fist on the desk. "Where's Leerie?"

"You can't have her—not this time." Miss Maxwell's lips became a fraction more firm, while her eyes sharpened into what her training girls had come to call her "forceps expression."

"Why not?"

"The girl's just off that case for Doctor Fritz; she's tired out. Remember she's been through three unbroken years of hospitals, and we've worked her on every hard case we've had since she came back. I'm going to see that she gets forty-eight hours of rest now."

"Let her have them next time." Doctor Fuller put all his persuasive charm into the words. "I need Leerie—some one who can roll up her sleeves and pitch in. Let me have her just this once."

But Miss Maxwell was obdurate. "She's asleep now, and she's going to sleep as long as she needs to. I'll give you Miss Grant—she's had a month at the Maternity at Rochester."

"A month!" Scorn curled up the ends of the doctor's mustache. The next instant they were almost touching in a broad grin. "Leerie likes cases like this—just eats them up. I'm going after her." And before the superintendent of nurses could hold him he was down the corridor on his way to the nurses' dormitory.

Ten minutes later he was back, grinning harder than ever. He had only time to thrust his head in the door and wave a triumphant arm. "She's dressing—as big a fool about babies as I am! Said she'd slept a whole hour and felt fresh as a daisy. How's that for spunk?"

"I call it nerve." Miss Maxwell smiled a hopeless smile. "What am I going to do with you doctors? You wear out all my best nurses and you won't take—" But Doctor Fuller had fled.

In spite of his boast of her, the baby specialist saw Sheila O'Leary visibly cringe when she took her first look at Pancho. He lay sprawling on his mother's bed in a room littered with hastily opened bags and trunks out of which had been pulled clothing of all kinds and hues. He had been relieved of the lace and pink ribbons and was swathed only in shirt and roundabout, his arms and legs projected like licorice sticks; being of the same color and very nearly the same thickness. He was dozing, tired out with the combination of much travel, screaming, shaking, and loss of breath. So wasted was he that the skin seemed drawn tight over temple and cheekbones; the eyes were pitifully sunken, and colorless lips fell back over toothless gums.

"How old is—it?" Sheila whispered at last.

"About nine months."

Sheila shuddered. "Just the adorable age. Ought to be all pink cheeks, dimples, and creases—and look at it!"

"I know, but wait. Give us time and we'll get some of those things started." Doctor Fuller wagged his head by way of encouragement.

Sheila answered with a deprecatory shake. "This time I don't believe you. That would be a miracle, and you can do about everything but miracles. Honestly, it doesn't seem as if I could touch it; looks about a thousand years old and just human enough to be horrible."

The old doctor eyed her askance. "Not going back on me, are you?"

"Of course I'm not, but there's no use in making believe it will be any joy-game. I'll be hating it every minute I'm on the case."

"Hate it as much as you like, only stick to it. Hello there, bub!" This to the brown atom, who was opening his eyes.

The eyes were large and brown and as soft and appealing as a baby seal's. For a moment they looked with strange, wondering intensity at the two figures bending over it, then with sudden doubling and undoubling of fists, a frantic upheaval of brown legs, the atom opened volcanically and poured forth scream after scream. It writhed, it clawed the air, it looked every whit as horrible as Sheila had claimed.

"Going to run?" the old doctor asked, anxiously.

For answer Sheila bent down lower and picked up the writhing mass. With a firm hand she braced it against her shoulder, patting it gently and swaying her body rhythmically to the patting. "Some eyes and some temper!" laughed Sheila. "Where's the mother?"

The screaming brought the corridor nurse to the door. "Where's the mother?" Sheila repeated.

The corridor nurse pointed to the strewn luggage and gave a contemptuous shrug. "Gone down to dinner looking like a bird of paradise. She said if the baby cried I was to stir up some of that milk from that can, mix it with water from that faucet, put it in that bottle, and feed it to him." Words failed to convey the outraged disgust in her voice.

The milk indicated was condensed milk in a half-emptied can; the bottle was the regulation kind for babies and as filthy as dirty glass could look. Sheila and Doctor Fuller exchanged glances.

"Plenty of fight in the little beggar or he wouldn't be outlasting—" The doctor swallowed the remainder of the sentence, cut short by a startled look on Sheila's face.

The screams had stopped a minute before, and Sheila believed the atom had dropped asleep. But instead of feeling the tiny body relax as a sleeping baby's will, it was growing slowly rigid. With this realization she strode to the bed and put the atom down. Before their eyes the body stiffened, while the head rolled slowly from side to side and under the half-closed lids the eyeballs rolled with it.

"Convulsions!" announced the corridor nurse, with an anxious look toward the door. Then, as a bell tinkled, she voiced her relief in a quick breath. "That's sixty-one. I'm hiking—"

"No, you don't!" The doctor jerked her back; he wanted to shake her. "You'll hustle some hot water for us, and then you'll stand by to hustle some more. See?" He was shedding all unnecessary clothing as he spoke, and Sheila was peeling the atom free of shirt and roundabout as fast as skilled fingers could move.

It is a wonderful thing to watch the fight between human skill and death for the life of a baby. So little it takes to swing the victory either way, so close does it border on the miraculous, that few can stand and see without feeling the silent, invisible presence of the Nazarene. A life thus saved seems to gather unto itself a special significance and value for those who have fought for it and those who receive it again. It creates new feelings and a clearer vision in blind, unthinking motherhood; it awakens to a vital response hitherto dormant fatherhood. And even the callous outsider becomes exalted with the wonder and closeness of that unseen presence.

As the brown atom writhed from one convulsion into another, Sheila and the old doctor worked with compressed lips and almost suspended breath; they worked like a single mind supplied with twice the usual amount of auxiliaries. They saw, without acknowledging it, the gorgeous, tropical figure that came and stood half-way between the door and the bed; lips carmined, throat and cheeks heavy with powder, jewels covering ears, neck, fingers, and wrists, she looked absurdly unreal beside the nurse in her uniform and the doctor in his shirt-sleeves. Occasionally Sheila glanced at her. If they won, would the mother care? The question came back to her consciousness again and again. In her own experience she knew how often the thing one called motherhood would come into actual existence after a struggle like this when birth itself had failed to accomplish anything but a physical obligation. Believing this, Sheila fought the harder.

After an hour the convulsions subsided. A few more drops of brandy were poured down the tiny throat, and slowly the heart took up its regulation work. Sheila wrapped the atom in a blanket, put it back on the bed, and beckoned to the mother.

Curiosity seemed to be the one governing emotion of the señora. She looked without any trace of grief, and, having looked, she spoke impassively: "I theenk eet dead. Yes?"

Doctor Fuller, with perspiration pouring from him, transfixed her with a stare. "No! That baby's going to get well now, and you're going to let Miss O'Leary teach you how to take proper care of it. Understand?" Then clapping his fellow-fighter on the back, he beamed down upon her. "Leerie, you're one grand soldier!"

The monotone of the gorgeous señora broke up any response Sheila might have given. "I theenk eet die, all the same," came the impassive voice. "The *padre* on the ship make it all ready for die—I theenk yes pret' soon."

"No!" The doctor fairly thundered it forth.

She stooped and pulled away a fold of the blanket with the tips of her fingers. "Eet look ver' ugly—like eet die. I theenk—all the same."

The doctor caught up his cast-off clothing and flung himself out of the room. Sheila watched him go, a faint smile pulling at the corners of her mouth. Strange! He had so evidently reached the end of his self-control, optimism, and patience, while she was just beginning to find hers. In the sweep of a second things looked wonderfully clear and hopeful. She thought she could understand what was in the mind and heart of the señora; what was more significant, she thought she could understand the reason for it. And what you can understand you can cope with.

She watched the señora searching in this trunk and that; she saw her jerk forth a diminutive dress of embroidery and fluted lace; while she thought the whole thing through to the finish and smiled one of her old inscrutable smiles.

"Pret' dress," said the señora. "Plent' lace and reebon. You put on for bury eet—I go find *padre*."

"No," said Sheila, emphatically, "you stay here. I'll go and find the *padre*."

She left them both in the charge of the corridor nurse and flew for the telephone. It took her less than a minute to get Father O'Friel; it took but a trifle more for her to outline her plan and bind him to it. And Father O'Friel, with a comprehension to match his conscientiousness, and a sense of humor to match them both, hardly knew whether to be shocked or amused.

"Why not appeal to the baby's father?"

"Realize it takes a month for a letter to reach that little South American ant-hill? Write now if you want to, but let me be trying my way while the letter is traveling."

"All right. But if it doesn't work—"

"It will. When my feelings about anything run all to the good this way, I'd bank anything on them. Now please hurry."

So it came about that instead of a burial service that night Father O'Friel conducted an original and unprecedented adoption ceremony. Without even a witness the señora signed a paper which she showed no inclination to read and which she would hardly have understood had she attempted it. It was enough for her that she could give away Francisco Enrique Manuel Machado y Rodriguez to a foolish nurse who was plainly anxious to be bothered with him. Death had seemed the only release from an obligation that exhausted and frightened her, and from which neither pleasure nor personal pride could be obtained. But this was another way mercifully held out to her, and she accepted it with gratitude and absolute belief. Eagerly she agreed to the conditions Sheila laid down; the father was to be notified and forced to make a life settlement on the atom; in the mean time she was to remain at the sanitarium, pay all expenses, and interfere in no way with the nurse or the baby. So desirous was she to display her gratitude that she heaped the atom's wardrobe—lace, ribbons, and embroidery—upon Sheila, and kissed the hem of Father O'Friel's cassock.

"*Qué gracioso—qué magnifico!*" Then she yawned behind her tinted nails. "I have ver' much the sleep. I find anothaire room and make what you call—*la cama.*" At the door she turned and cast a farewell look upon the blanketed bundle. "Eet look ver' ugly—all the same I theenk eet die."

It took barely ten minutes for word of the adoption to reach Doctor Fuller, and it brought him running. "Good Lord! Leerie, are you crazy? Did you think I pulled you out of bed to-night to start an orphan-asylum? What do you mean, girl?"

Sheila looked down at her newly acquired possession, and for the first time that night the strange, luminous look that was all her own, that had won for her her nickname of Leerie, crept into her eyes; they fairly dazzled the old doctor with their shining. "Honestly, don't know myself. Still testing out my feelings in my think laboratory."

"You can't raise that baby and keep on with your nursing. Too much responsibility, anyway, for a young person. What's more, the mother shouldn't be allowed to dodge it. She can be made fit."

"How are you going to do it? Train her with harness and braces? Or moral suasion—or the courts?"

"And I thought you hated it, couldn't bear to touch it," growled the baby specialist.

"Did. But that's past tense. Since I fought for it, it's suddenly become remarkably precious. And that's the precise feeling I'm testing up in the lab."

"In the name of common sense what do you mean, Leerie?"

She patted his arm soothingly. "There, there. Go to bed; you're tuckered out. Leave me alone for two months, and I'll tell you. And suppose you write down that milk formula before you go; he's going to wake up as fighting hungry as a little tiger-cat."

How the sanitarium took the news of the arrivals and the rumor of the adoption, what they thought of the gorgeous and irresponsible señora and Leerie's latest exploit, does not concern the story. It is enough to say that tongues wagged abundantly; and when Sheila appeared some ten days later in the pine grove wheeling a perambulator every one who was out and could manufacture the flimsiest excuse for her curiosity hurried to the carriage and thrust an inquisitive head under the hood. It seemed as if hundreds blocked the walk from the pond to the rest-house.

"Bad as a circus parade," thought Sheila. "Can't stay here, or they'll put us in a tent and ask admission." Then she spied Hennessy coming with his platter of bread for the swans, and called to him. Somehow he managed to scatter the crowd, and Sheila clung to the sleeve of his blue jumper as if it had been so much cork to a man overboard. "Listen, Hennessy, I want to take Pancho away from the San. You and Marm have a cozy place, and it's far enough away. There's only the two of you. Can't you take us in?"

But Hennessy was likewise thrusting a head under the hood. "Honest to God, Miss Leerie, is it human?"

"Hennessy, don't be an idiot!"

"But I saw the face on it—an' the scratchin' it did the day it was fetched in. Does it still be scratchin'?"

"Sometimes." Sheila smiled faintly. "He hasn't had time yet to forget all those shakings. Well, can we come?"

Hennessy eyed the perambulator fearsomely. "Have to ask Marm. Faith, do ye think, now, if it had been human, its mother would have given it away same as if it had been a young cat or dog too many in the litter?"

"Mothers don't have to love their babies; there's no birth license to sign, you know, with a love-and-cherish clause in it. Just come, wanted or not, and afterward—"

But Hennessy was deep in speculations of his own. "Now if it was Ireland, Miss Leerie, do ye know what I would be thinkin'?"

"What?"

He lowered his voice and looked furtively over his shoulder. "A changeling! Sure as you're born, Miss Leerie, I'm thinkin' it's one o' them little black imps the fairies leave in place o' the real child they're after stealin'. I disremember if they have the likes o' that in South America, but that's my notion, just the same."

Sheila O'Leary laughed inside and out. "Hennessy, you're wonderful. And who but an Irishman would have thought of it! A changeling—a most changeable changeling! What's the treatment?"

"A good brewin' of egg-shells—goose egg-shells if ye have 'em, hens' if ye haven't. But don't ye be laughin'; 'tis a sign o' black doin's, an' laughin' might bring bad luck on ye."

Sheila sobered. "We'll brew egg-shells. Now hurry home to Marm and coax her hard, Hennessy."

Because Sheila O'Leary invariably had her way among the many who loved and believed in her, and because Hennessy and Marm Hennessy were numbered conspicuously among these, Sheila and her adopted moved early the following morning into the diminutive and immaculate house of Hennessy, with a vine-covered porch in front and a hen-yard in the rear. And that night there was a plentiful brew of egg-shells on the kitchen stove, done in the most approved Irish fashion, with the atom near by to inhale the fumes.

"Maybe 'twill work, an' then again maybe 'twon't." Hennessy looked anxious. "Magic, like anything else, often spoils in transportatin'."

"Oh, it will work!" Sheila spoke with conviction. "And we'll hope the señora's letter won't travel too fast."

So the names of Sheila O'Leary and Francisco Enrique Manuel Machado y Rodriguez were crossed off the books of the sanitarium, and the gossips saw them no more. Only Doctor Fuller and Peter Brooks sought them out in their new quarters, the doctor to attend professionally, Peter to attend to the dictates of a persistent heart. Never a day went by that he did not find his feet trailing the dust on the road to the house of Hennessy, and Sheila dropped into the habit of watching for him from the vine-covered porch at a certain time every afternoon. The picture of the best nurse at the sanitarium sitting in a little old rocker with the brown atom kicking and crowing on her lap, and looking down the steps with eyes that seemed to grow daily more luminous, came to be an accepted reality to both Peter and the doctor—as much of a reality as the reaching out of the atom's small tendril-like fingers to curl about one's thumb or to cling to one's watch-charm.

"Loving little cuss," muttered Peter one afternoon. "Can you tell me how any mother under the sun could resist those eyes or the clutch of those brown paws?"

"Don't forget one point," Sheila spoke quietly; "he wasn't a loving little cuss then."

"He'll go down on the books as my pet case," chuckled the doctor. "Four pounds in four weeks! Think of it, on a whole-milk formula!"

Hennessy wagged his head knowingly at Sheila, and when they had gone he snorted forth his contempt for professional ignorance. "Milk! Fiddlesticks! Sure a docthor don't know everything. 'Twas the egg-shells that done it, an' Marm an' me can bear witness he quit the scratchin' an' began the smilin' from that very hour. Look at him now! Can ye deny it, Miss Leerie?"

"I'm not wanting to, Hennessy." Whereupon Sheila proved the matter by reducing the atom to squeals of joy while she retold the old history of the pigs with the aid of five little brown toes.

Between Peter and Hennessy, Sheila came into possession of many facts concerning the señora. Her dresses and her jewels were the talk of the sanitarium. She applied herself diligently to all beautifying treatments and the charming of susceptible young men. Presumably life to her meant only a continuous process of adorning herself and receiving admiration. So she spent her days dressing and basking in the company of a dozen different swains, and the atom cast no annoying shadow on her pathway.

August came, and the atom discovered his legs. Sheila disregarded the lace and ribbons with a sigh of relief and took to making rompers. They were adorable rompers with smocking and the palest of pink collars and belts. The licorice sticks had changed to a rich olive brown and had assumed sufficient rotundity to allow of pink-and-white socks and white ankle-ties. In all the busy years of her nursing Sheila had never had time for anything like this; she had never had a baby for longer than a week or two at a time. Just as she was beginning to feel her individual share in them they had all gone the way of properly parented offspring, and never had she sewed a single baby dress. She gloried in the lengths of dimity and poplin, in the intricacies of new stitches and embroidery. And Peter, watching from a step on the porch, gloried in the picture she made.

When a romper was finished it had to be tried on that very minute. She would whisk up the atom from the hammock where he lay kicking, and slip him into it, holding him high for Peter to admire.

"He's a cherub done in bronze," said Peter, one day. "Here, give him to me." And later, as he perched him on his shoulder and tickled his ribs until he squirmed with glee he announced, "If I wasn't a homeless bachelor I'd take him off your hands in about two minutes."

"What's that?" shouted Doctor Fuller, coming down the street. "Did you say anything about re-adoption? Well, you might as well know now that Mrs. Fuller and I intend taking Pancho off Leerie's hands as soon as she's ready to go back to work again. Aren't you getting lazy, Leerie?"

For once Sheila failed to respond in kind to the doctor's chaffing. All the shine faded out of her eyes. "Can't believe two months have gone—a month for a letter to go, a month for an answer to come. I'm afraid none of us will keep him very much longer."

"Don't worry, they won't want him back. Besides, they've forfeited their right to him," the old doctor snorted, indignantly.

Holding him high for Peter to admire

"Not legally. When the letter comes, you'll see." There was none of the anticipated delight in Sheila's voice that had been there on that first night when she had laid her plans and sworn Father O'Friel into backing her up. Her voice was as colorless as her eyes were dull; for some miraculous reason the life and inner light that seemed such an inseparable part of her had suddenly gone out. She reached up and removed the atom from Peter's shoulder.

Hennessy, who had joined the group, was the last to speak. "Sure it's mortial good of both ye gentlemen to lift the throuble o' raisin' the wee one off Miss Leerie, but if any one lifts it, it's Marm an' me. We had that settled the next morning after we fetched him over an' knew 'twas the real one we'd got, after all."

"The real one? What do you mean by that?" The doctor looked puzzled.

Hennessy winked his only answer.

Through the first days of September Sheila waited with feverish anxiety. The hours spent on the vine-covered porch with the atom, asleep or awake, for steady company, and Peter for occasional, passed all too quickly. For the first time in her life Sheila wished days back; she would have put a checking hand on time had she had the power. Then just as she was making up her mind that her fear was for nothing, that her plans had gloriously failed and Pancho was to be hers for all time, the wretched news came. Peter brought it, hurrying hatless down the street, and Sheila, knowing in her heart what had happened, went down the steps to meet him.

"Is it a letter—or a wire—or what? And where's the señora?"

"Having hysterics in front of the business office." Peter stopped to get his breath. "The husband wired from New York—he'll be down on the morning train. It seems the señora wired him when she first got here that Pancho was dying, so she didn't see any need of changing it in her letter. She said she wanted the money for a monument and masses—and he could send it in a draft. Guess he thought more of the boy than the mother did, for he's come up to bring the body home and put up the monument down there. Now she doesn't know what to tell him. Can you beat that for straight fiction?"

Sheila picked up the atom and disappeared inside without a word. When she reappeared a few minutes later, the atom was arrayed in his most becoming romper, his black curls were brushed into an encircling halo, his hands clapping over some consciousness of pleasurable excitement. Sheila tucked him into his carriage and faced Peter with a grim look of command. "You're to play policeman, understand! Walk back of me all the way. If I show any sign of turning back or running away, arrest me on the spot."

"What are you going to do?"

"What two months ago I thought would be the easiest thing in the world—and what I wouldn't be doing now for a million dollars if I hadn't given my word to Father O'Friel and the law wasn't against me."

As Peter had rightfully reported, the señora was having hysterics in front of the business office, with the business and hospital staff trying their best to quench her, and as many patients as the lobby would hold watching in varying degrees of curiosity. Only one of Latin blood could have achieved a scene of such melodramatic abandon and stamped it as genuine, but no one present doubted the grief and despair of the señora as she paced the floor wringing her hands and wailing in her native tongue. Sheila entered by way of the basement and the lift, and she wheeled the atom's carriage into the inner circle of the crowd, with Peter still in attendance.

For the moment the interest swerved from the weeping figure to the cooing occupant of the carriage. The atom was still clapping his hands, and a pink flush of excitement tinged the olive of the cheeks. "Look at that cunning baby!"... "Isn't he a darling?"... "Why, isn't that the South American baby?"... "Sh-h-h—deformed or something."... "Of course, it can't be." Sentences, whole and in fragments, came to Sheila as she pushed her way through the crowd.

Something of this new interest must have penetrated the señora's consciousness, for her wailing ceased; she cocked her head on one side like a listening parrakeet. "Who say babee? I theenk—I theenk—" Then she saw Sheila. A look of immediate recognition swept over her face, but it was gone the instant she looked at the atom. "Who that babee?" she demanded.

"Mine." Sheila pinned her with steady eyes, while her mouth looked as if it could never grow gentle and demure again.

Incredulity, suspicion, amazement, were all registered on the pretty, shallow face. "Your babee? How you get babee?"

Sheila made no answer.

The señora looked again at the atom; she held out a timorous finger to him. He responded cordially by curling a small fist promptly about it. "*Madre de Dios, qué bonito! Qué chico y hermoso!*" Then, to Sheila: "I give you seeck babee—eet no die? You make thees babee out of seeck babee, yes?"

Sheila still remained silent.

The señora turned to the atom for the confirmation she desired. "*Nene, como te llamas?*"

It was intensely entertaining to the atom. He wagged the señora's finger frantically, tossed back his head, and gave forth a low, gurgling laugh. "*Jesu!* That ees hees papa. He look like that when he laugh. *Tu nombre, nene—tu nombre?*" With a fresh outburst she sank down beside the carriage and buried her face in the brown legs and pink socks.

But the atom did not approve of this. His lower lip dropped and quivered; he reached out his arm to Sheila. "Ma-ma-ma-ma," he coaxed.

"You no ma-ma, I ma-ma." The señora was on her feet, shaking an angry fist at Sheila. But in an instant her anger was gone; she was down on her knees again, clasping Sheila's skirt, while her voice wailed forth in supplication. "You no keep leetle babee? You ver' good, ver' kind, señorita—you *muy simpatica*, yes? You give leetle babee. I ma-ma. Yes?"

But Sheila O'Leary stood grim and unyielding. "No. He is mine. When he was sick, dying, you didn't want him. You did not like to look at him because he was ugly; you did not like to hear him cry—so you abused him. Now, he's all well; he's a pretty baby; he does not cry; he does not scratch. I never shake him; he loves me very, very much. Now I keep him!" Thus Sheila delivered her ultimatum.

But the señora still clung. "I no shake babee now. I love babee now. Please—please—his pa-pa come. You give heem back?"

Sheila unclasped the señora's hands, turned the atom's carriage about, and deliberately wheeled him away.

Out of the lobby to the sidewalk she was pursued by pleading cries, expostulating reproofs, as well as actual particles of the crowd itself, the Reverend Mr. Grumble, the wife of one of the trustees, a handful of protesting patients, following to urge the rights of the prostrated mother. But Sheila refused to be held back or argued with; stoically she kept on her way. When she reached the little vine-covered porch only Peter, Father O'Friel, and Doctor Fuller remained as escort.

"You can't keep him, Leerie. You've got to give him up." The old doctor spoke sorrowfully but firmly.

"It was only a mock adoption, and you promised if she ever wanted him back she should have him," Father O'Friel reminded her.

"She's his mother, after all," Peter put in, lamely.

At that Sheila exploded. "You men make me tired! 'She's his mother, after all.' After all what? Cruelty, neglect, heartlessness, hoping he would die—glad to be rid of him! That's about all the sense of justice you have. Let a woman weep and call for her baby, and every man within earshot would hand him over without considering for a moment what kind of care she would give him. Oh, you—make—me—sick!" Sheila buried her face in the nape of Pancho's neck.

Doctor Fuller, who had always known her, who had stood by her in her disgrace when she had been sent away from the sanitarium three years before and had believed in her implicitly in spite of all damning evidence, who had fought for her a dozen times when she had called down upon her head the wrath of the business office, looked now upon her silent, shaking figure with open-mouthed astonishment. In all those years he had never seen Leerie cry, and he couldn't quite stand it.

"There, there, child! We understand—we're not quite the duffers you make us out. Of course, by all rights, human and moral, the little shaver belongs to you, but you can't keep him, just the same."

"Know it! Needn't rub it in! Wasn't going to!" Sheila raised a wet face, with red-rimmed eyes and lips that trembled outrageously. She couldn't steady them to save her, and so she let them tremble while she stuttered forth her last protest. "Didn't think for a moment I wouldn't give him back, d-d-did you? That was my plan—my way. I wanted Father O'Friel to let me try—t-t-t-thought all along he'd grow into such an ad-d-d-dorable mite his m-m-m-mother'd be wanting him back. What I didn't count on was my wanting to k-k-keep him." Sheila swallowed hard. She wanted to get rid of that everlasting choke in her throat. When she spoke again her voice was steadier. "But I tell you one thing. She doesn't get him without fighting for him. She's going to fight for him as I fought that night in the sanitarium, and you're going to help me keep her fighting. Understand? Then perhaps when she gets him she'll have some faint notion of how precious a baby can be." With a more grim expression than any of the three had ever seen on her usually luminous face, Sheila O'Leary shouldered the atom and disappeared within the house.

The three men stood by her while Hennessy guarded the house. For the rest of the day the señora, backed by the business office and a procession of interested sympathizers, stormed the parish house and demanded to see the paper that she had signed. They stormed Doctor Fuller's office and demanded his co-operation, or at least what information he had to give. They consulted the one lawyer in the town and three others within car distance, but their advice availed little, inasmuch as Father O'Friel had refused to give up the paper until the baby's father arrived, and they could get no intelligent idea from the señora of how legal the adoption had been made. By keeping perfectly dumb the three were able to hold the crowd in abeyance, and the señora, looking anything but a bird of paradise, came back to them again and again to weep, to plead, to bribe.

The excitement held until midnight, an unprecedented occurrence for the sanitarium. It was still dark the next morning when Hennessy was roused from the haircloth sofa in the hall, where he was still keeping guard, by the fumbling of a hand on the door-knob. "Who's there?" roared Hennessy.

"Please—eet ees me—the Señora Machado y Rodriguez."

"Go 'way! Shoo-oo!" Hennessy banged the door with his fist as he always banged the bread-platter to scatter the swans.

"I go when I see babee," came the feeble response to his racket.

"Let her in, Hennessy," came the voice of Sheila from up-stairs.

Hennessy unbarred the door, and a shaken, pathetic little figure crept in. All the coy prettiness was gone for the moment; the swollen eyes had circles about them, the cheeks were sallow and free of powder as the lips were free of carmine. The mouth quivered like a grief-stricken child's. "Please—please—I see babee?" came the wail again.

"Yes. Come up softly," Sheila called from the head of the stairs.

The little figure crept up eagerly. Sheila put out an arm and led her into a room where a single candle burned beside the bed. There lay the atom, rosy and dimpling in his sleep.

It is to be doubted if the señora had ever dreamed of such a possession after the appalling reality of the original Francisco Enrique Manuel Machado y Rodriguez. In her ignorance and youth she had accepted ugliness, sickness, and peevish crying as the normal attributes of babyhood, and because of this she had loathed it. Therefore to be suddenly confronted with her awful mistake, to find that she had thrown away something that was beautiful and enchanting, to know she had forfeited what might have been hers, to feel in a small degree the first longing of motherhood and be denied it—all this was born into the slowly awakening consciousness of the señora. It almost transformed her face into homely holiness as she made her one supreme prayer and sacrifice. "You give me my babee—now—you give heem and not keep—and I give you all these. See?" She held out her hands that had been clasped under the heavy mantilla that covered her head and shoulders. Opening them, she thrust them close, that Sheila might look. They were filled with jewels—the jewels she adored, that had contributed a large part to the joy of her existence. Pins, rings, necklaces, bracelets—the señora had not kept back a single ornament. "You—you and the blessed Maria will give heem back to me?"

"Get down and pray to the Maria," commanded Sheila. "Promise her that if she will give your baby back to you you will take care of him for ever and ever. Never neglect him, never shake nor slap him, never give him bad milk to make him sick. Promise you'll always love him and keep him laughing and pretty. And remember—break your promise, let anything happen to Pancho again, and Maria will not give him back to you another time."

The sanitarium never learned in detail how Señor Machado became reconciled to a live son, not being present when the news was conveyed to him. They saw him arrive, however, looking very much shaken with his bereavement, and they saw him depart with his son perched high upon his shoulder, wearing the expression of one who has come unexpectedly into a great possession, while the señora clung to them both. The sanitarium waved them off with gladness and satisfaction—all but four unsmiling outsiders. So great a hole can a departing atom sometimes leave behind that those four who had given him temporary care and guardianship went about for days with sorrow written plainly upon them. Hennessy fed the swans in bitter silence; Peter moped, with a laugh for no one; Doctor Fuller groaned whenever South America was mentioned; while all three knew they could not even fathom the deepness or the bigness of that hole for Sheila.

Peter took her for a twilight ride in his car the first empty night. "Go on and cry it out—I sha'n't mind," he urged as he speeded the car along a country road.

Sheila smiled faintly. "Thank you—can't. Just feel bruised and banged all over—feel as if I needed a plunge in that old pool of Bethesda."

They spun on in silence for a few miles more before Sheila spoke again. "I learned one wonderful thing from Pancho—something I never felt sure of before."

"What was that?"

"Sorry—can't tell. It's the sort of thing you tell only the man you marry, after you've discovered he's the only man you ever could have married."

Peter speeded the car ahead and smiled quietly into the gathering darkness. Fortunately he was not an impatient man.

There is one point concerning the atom that Hennessy and Doctor Fuller still wrangle over, neither of them having the slightest conception of the other's point of view.

"That was a case of good nursing and milk," the old doctor persists.

While Hennessy beats the air with his fists and shouts: "Nothing of the sort! 'Twas egg-shells that done it."

Chapter IV

FOR THE HONOR OF THE SAN

PETER BROOKS paced the sanitarium grounds like a man possessed. Hands thrust deep into pockets, teeth hard clenched, head bare, the raw October wind ruffling his heavy crop of hair like a cock's comb. So suggestive was the resemblance that Hennessy, watching him from the willow stump by the pond, was forced to remark to Brian Boru, the gray swan, that Mr. Peter looked like a young rooster, after growing his spurs, looking for his first fight.

"Aye, an' for one I'm wishin' he'd be findin' it," continued Hennessy. "He's bided peaceful an' patient till there is no virtue left in him. Ye can make believe women be civilized if ye like, but I'm knowin' that a woman's sure to go to the man that fights the hardest to get her, same as it was in the savage day o' the world. An' there's nothing that sets a man right quicker with himself than a good fight, tongues or fists."

At that moment Peter would have gladly chosen either or both if fate could only have furnished him with a legitimate combatant. But a man cannot fight gossipy old ladies or jealous, petty-minded nurses, or a doctor whom he has never met and whose transgressions he cannot swear to. And yet Peter wanted to double up his fists and pitch into the whole community; he felt himself all brute and yearned for wholesale slaughter.

Peter had come to the sanitarium in the beginning to be cured of a temporal malady, only to rise from his bed stricken with an eternal one. He had fallen desperately in love with Sheila O'Leary as only a man of Peter's sort can fall in love, once and for all time. Moreover, he believed in her as a man believes in the best and purest that is likely to come into his life. On the day of his convalescing, when she had been transferred from his case to another, he had sworn that he would not stir foot from the old San until he had won her. He had kept his word for four months. He would have been content to keep it for four more—or for four years, for that matter—had everything not turned suddenly topsy-turvy and sent his world of hopes crashing down about him.

For four months he had shared as much of Sheila's life and work as she would allow. He had let himself drift into the rôle of a comfortable and sympathetic companion whenever her hours for recreation gave him a chance. His love had grown as his admiration and understanding of her had grown, until she had come to seem as necessary a part of his life as the air he breathed. Then he had been able to smile whimsically at those gossipy tales. What if she had been suspended and sent away from the sanitarium? What if she had broken through some of the tight-laced rules with which all institutions of this kind hedge in their nurses? Sheila's proclivity for breaking rules was a byword among the many who loved her, and the head of the institution, the superintendent of nurses, the entire staff of doctors, down to Hennessy, the keeper of the walks and swans, only smiled and closed their eyes to all of Sheila's backsliding. For hadn't they all believed in her? And hadn't they sent for her to come back to them again? And which one of them had ever allowed a word of scandal to pass his lips? So Peter smiled, too.

In those months he had come to read Sheila—so he thought—like an open book. He had learned by heart all her moods, the good and the bad, the sweet and the bitter. He knew she could be as divinely tender and compassionate as a celestial mother; he also knew that she could be as barren of sympathy and as relentless as fate itself. She could pour forth her whole throbbing soul, impulsive, warm, and radiant, as a true Celt, yet she could be as impersonal, terse, and cryptic as a marconigram. He loved these very extremes in her, her unmitigated hatred for the things she hated, and her unfailing love for the things she loved. She made no pretense or boast for herself; she was what she was for all the world to see. And Peter had found her the stanchest, sweetest, most vital—albeit the most stubborn—piece of womanhood he had ever known. Her very nickname of "Leerie" was her open letter of introduction to every one; her smile and the wonder-light in her eyes were her best credentials. Small wonder it was that her patients watched for her to come and that Peter felt he could snap his fingers at the scandalmongers.

But Peter wasn't snapping them now—or smiling. His fists were doubled tight in his pockets, and he clenched his teeth harder as he paced the walk from pond to rest-house. How the accursed tongues of the gossips rang in his head! "Rather odd the sanitarium should have sent for him, wasn't it? Don't you know he was the young surgeon who was mixed up in that affair with that popular nurse?"... "Oh yes, they hushed it up and sent them both away."... "Nothing definite was ever explained, but they were always together, just as they are now, and you can't get smoke without some burning."... "Yes, Doctor Brainard and Miss O'Leary. Didn't you ever hear about what happened three years ago?"

Peter's stride seemed to measure forth the length of each offending tongue, and when he reached the end of his beaten track he swung about as if to meet and silence them all, for all time. But instead he came face to face with the two who had caused them to wag. So absorbed were the surgeon and nurse in what they had to say to each other that they brushed by Peter without seeing him. He might have been one of the rustic posts of the rest-house or the pine-tree growing close by. As they passed, Peter scanned narrowly the half-averted face of the girl he loved and found it pitifully changed in those few days. The luminous light had gone from her eyes; her lips no longer curved to the gracious, demure smile Peter had always called "cloistered." They were set to grim determination, as if the girl had gripped fast to a purpose and no amount of shaking or persuasion would induce her to let go. Her eyes were circled and anxious. Peter groaned unconsciously at his glimpse of her, while Hennessy from his vantage-point on the stump shook a vengeful fist at the retreating back of the surgeon.

"A million curses on him!" muttered Hennessy, his lips tight shirred. "Sure, the lass has the look of a soul possessed." The next instant his fist was descending not over-mercifully on Peter's back. "First I'm cursin' him an' then I'm cursin' ye. For the love o' Saint Patrick, are ye goin' to stand round like a blitherin' fool an' see that rascal of a docthor do harm again to our lass? I'll come mortial close to wringin' your neck if ye do."

Peter glared at his erstwhile friend and fellow-philosopher. "You're the fool, Hennessy. What under heaven can I do? What could any man do in my place?"

"Fight for her. Can't you see the man has her possessed? What an' how Hennessy hasn't the wits to make out, but ye have. Search out her throuble same as she searched out yours, an' make her whole an' sweet an' shinin' again." Hennessy laid two gnarled, brown hands on Peter's shoulder while he peered up at him with eyes full of appeal. "Ye've heard naught to shake your faith in the lass? Ye believe in her—aye?"

"Good God! man, of course I believe in her! I'd believe in her if all the tongues in the world wagged till doomsday. But what else can I do? Hang around this old hotbed of gossip and listen and listen, powerless to cram the truth down their throats because I don't know it?" Peter shot out a sudden hand and gripped Hennessy's. "For the love of your blessed Saint Patrick, stand up like a man there, Hennessy, and tell me what was the truth?"

For a moment Hennessy's eyes shifted; he whistled his breath in and out in staccato jerks; then his gaze came back to Peter and he eyed him steadily. "Son, I'm knowin' no more than when I first saw ye."

"You believe in her?"

Hennessy pulled his hand free and shook his fist in Peter's face. "Bad scran to ye for thinkin' aught else. 'Tis God's truth I'm tellin' ye, Mr. Peter. I'm knowin' no more than them blitherin' tongues say, but I'd pray our lass into heaven wi' my dyin' breath if I could."

Peter smiled. "You'd be doing better to pray her out of this miserable little purgatory right here. If she belonged to me, Hennessy—"

"I wish to God she did, sir! But that's what ye can fight for—make her belong."

"Easier said than done. Since Doctor Brainard came I can't get her to see me. Read that!" Peter pulled out of his pocket a tiny folded note and handed it to the swan-keeper. It was deciphered with much labor and read with troubled seriousness.

Dear Mr. Brooks:

Thank you for the flowers, and the candy, and the many offers of the car, but I haven't time to enjoy any of these things just now. So please don't send me any more, or write, or try to see me. I think it would be better for every one, and far happier in the end for you, if you would go back to your work as soon as possible.

    Faithfully yours,
    SHEILA O'LEARY.

Hennessy snorted. "So that's what she thinks, is it? Well, don't ye do it. 'Twas betther advice I gave ye myself; hold fast here an' fight for her. Mind that!" And with a farewell pull of his forelock Hennessy left him.

Peter watched him for an instant, then with a new purpose full-born in his mind he turned and walked swiftly back to the sanitarium. He knew why the management had sent for Brainard to come back to the San. The head surgeon had been taken with typhoid; the wards were full of his special operative cases, and Brainard, who had trained under him, was the most skilful man available to take his place. But why had they put Sheila O'Leary on as his surgical nurse? Why had they done this thing that was bound to revive the old scandal and set tongues wagging anew? Peter knew that upon the answer to this depended his decision. Would he take Sheila's advice and go, or Hennessy's advice and fight?

He went directly to the office of the superintendent of nurses, and, finding the door well ajar, he entered without knocking. Miss Maxwell was seated at her desk. Across the desk, with clasped hands, cheeks aflame, and lips compressed into a look of even greater determination than Peter had seen there a few minutes before, leaned Sheila O'Leary.

Peter colored at his unintentional intrusion. "Excuse me," he stammered. "Not hearing voices, I thought you were alone. I'll come again later, Miss Maxwell," and he turned toward the door.

Leerie's voice called him back. "Don't go—want you. Something I was trying to get Miss Max to promise."

This time Miss Maxwell colored. "It's against rules, Leerie, to talk over hospital matters before patients, even as discreet a one as Mr. Brooks."

"I know—can't help it—need him. Besides, he's his best friend." She turned to Peter with a strained eagerness. "This will be news to you. Doctor Dempsy is due here in the morning—taken suddenly—major operation—nurse just wired. I want you and Miss Max to take him on to the Dentons if he can stand the trip. Awfully delicate operation, and it's Doctor John's crack piece of work. Will you do it?"

The unexpectedness of the news and the request overwhelmed Peter's usually agile intelligence. He stared blankly at the girl before him. "I don't think I understand. If Dempsy is coming here for an operation, why should we take him somewhere else? Why shouldn't he be operated on here if he wants to be?"

"He thinks Doctor Jefferson is still operating. He doesn't know—"

The superintendent of nurses interrupted her. "Leerie, you're overstepping even your privileges. Doctor Brainard was called here to take charge because the management had absolute confidence in his skill and knew he was trustworthy and conscientious. I think there is nothing further that needs to be said. Doctor Dempsy will do what every other patient has done, put himself unreservedly into Doctor Brainard's hands."

"But he mustn't." The crimson had died out of Sheila's cheeks, and she stood now pale to the very lips, her face working convulsively. "You don't seem to understand, and it's hard—hard to put it into words. Doctor Brainard is young—very young for his position and all the responsibility that has been heaped upon him. His work ever since he came has been terrific—eight and ten majors a day, Sundays, too. It's been a fearful strain, and now to make him responsible for a case like Doctor Dempsy, a case that takes great delicacy and nerve, one that is bound to attack his sympathy and his reputation at the same time, why—why, it isn't fair. Can't you see that if he should fail, no matter how blameless he might be, it would stick to him for the rest of his life, a blot on his work and the San?" Sheila's hands went out in a last appeal. "Send him to the Dentons; they've had five years of experience for every year of Doctor Brainard's. Please, please! Oh, don't you see?"

"Why should you care so much?" The words were off Peter's tongue before he knew it. He would have given a good deal if he could have got them back.

The girl looked from him to Miss Maxwell. The question apparently bewildered her. Then a hint of her old-time dignity and assurance returned, coupled with her cryptic mood. "Plenty of reasons: he was Miss Max's chief—she always worshiped him—your best friend, a most loved and honored man in the profession. Isn't he? Well, this isn't the time or the place for a risk."

The superintendent rose and looked down at the girl. When she spoke there was a touch of annoyance in the tone as well as sadness. "And that's as much—and as little—as you expect to tell us?"

Sheila nodded.

Miss Maxwell threw up her hands in a little gesture of helplessness. "Leerie, Leerie, what are we going to do with you? It was this way even three years ago."

In a flash the girl's arms were about the superintendent's neck, her face buried on her shoulder; the words were barely audible to Peter, "Love me and believe in me—as you did three years ago." And then a choking, wet-eyed, and rather disheveled figure flew past him, out of the room.

Miss Maxwell sank back heavily into her chair; her face showed plainly her battling between love for the girl, her sense of outraged discipline, and her anxiety over the decision she must make. Peter watched her with a sort of impersonal sympathy; the major part of his being had been plunged into what seemed a veritable chasm of hopelessness. He tried to pull himself together and realize that there was Dempsy to think about.

"What are you going to do?" he asked, at last.

"Do? You mean—about—?"

Peter nodded.

An almost pathetic smile crept into the superintendent's face. "As long as you were here, anyway, it's rather a relief to be able to confess that I don't know what to do. You see, superintendents are always supposed to have infallible judgment on all matters," she sighed. "I have never but once known Leerie to break a rule or ask for a special dispensation without a reason—a good reason. But I don't understand what lies behind all this."

"I do." Peter fairly roared it forth. "She loves that man, and she's afraid this might ruin his career if—if anything happened. Why, it's as plain as these four walls and the ceiling above us. No woman pleads for a man that way unless she loves him better than anything else on God's earth."

"I think you're wrong."

"Why?" Peter strode over to the superintendent's desk like a man after his reprieve. "I'm not just curious. I've the biggest excuse in the world for wanting to know why she has asked this. I love Sheila O'Leary. I love her well enough to leave her to-night with the man she loves, provided he loves her. But if he doesn't—if he's just playing with her, accepting her as a sop to his vanity, as a lot of near-famous men will with a woman—then, by thunder! I'm going to stay and fight him for her! Understand?" And Peter's fist pounded the desk.

The superintendent smiled again. This time there was no pathos in it. "I understand—and I'd stay. You ought to know Leerie well enough by this time to know that she can fight for the right of anything, whether she cares personally or not, and more than that, even if she has to suffer for it herself. She's the only woman I have ever known who had that particular kind of heroism. If she felt Doctor Brainard needed some one to stand up for him, I believe she could plead better if she didn't care. And I've another, a better reason for thinking she doesn't love him. She refused at first to be his surgical nurse. She didn't consent until she knew that he had made that one of the conditions of his coming here; he stipulated that he must be allowed to bring his own anesthetist, operate without an assistant, and choose his own operating nurse."

"And he choose her?"

"She is the best we have. Not using an assistant throws a tremendous responsibility and strain on the nurse, and Doctor Brainard naturally wanted the most expert one he could get."

"Then there was nothing personal—"

"I don't think so. Doctor Brainard has a strong influence over Leerie, but I believe it is only what any surgeon with distinction and power would have. If she really cared for Doctor Brainard, she wouldn't have said what she did when I asked her to take the appointment."

"What did she say?" Peter leaned forward eagerly and gripped the edge of the desk.

"She said she would rather be suspended for three more years than do it, but if there was no one else, she guessed she could manage it for the honor of the San."

"What did she mean?"

"Oh, that's just a by-phrase among those of us who have worked here a long while and feel a certain loyalty and responsibility for the ideals of this institution. We have tried to stand for honest, humane work as against mere moneygrubbing and popularity."

"I see. That's why Dempsy sent me here; that's why he's coming himself. Thank you, Miss Maxwell. I hope you're right." Peter straightened himself and moved toward the door.

"Wait a minute, Mr. Brooks. How much do you know of what happened three years ago?"

"Just what has dripped from the wagging tongues." Peter smiled ironically.

"Suppose I tell you the truth of it. It might help you to fight this thing through. It certainly couldn't hurt your love for Leerie if you really love her."

"Nothing could," said Peter, simply.

"Doctor Brainard and Leerie were the very best of friends during the years she was training and he was working under Doctor Jefferson. Then I thought it was love; they were always together, and there seemed to be a strong, deep sympathy between the two. Just about the time she graduated things began to go awry. Doctor Brainard was on the verge of a nervous breakdown and Leerie seemed to be laboring under some bad mental strain. Then the nurses began to hint that Leerie had been going to his room. One night, when she was head night nurse in the Surgical and Miss Jacobs was fourth corridor nurse, Miss Jacobs called me up at two in the morning and told me Leerie had been in Doctor Brainard's room for an hour. I came at once and found her there. She made no explanation, offered no excuses. She even acknowledged that she had been there twice before at the same time."

"What did Brainard say?" Peter asked it through clenched teeth.

"Nothing then. But later, when he was called before the Board, he laughed and asked what a man could say when a nurse chose to come to his room at two in the morning."

"The cad!" and Peter swore under his breath.

"I should have believed in Leerie, anyway, but it was that laugh of Doctor Brainard's that made me determined to fight for her. What motive Doctor Brainard had for not defending her I don't know, but he acted like a scoundrel."

"But why?" Peter beat the air. "Oh, the girl must have known she couldn't run amuck with convention that way and not have it hurt her! Why did she do it?"

The superintendent of nurses looked long and thoughtfully at him. "Do you know, Mr. Brooks, if I happened to be the man who loved Sheila O'Leary, I think I'd find that out as soon as I could. The answer might prove valuable; it might solve the riddle why Sheila doesn't want Doctor Dempsy operated on here."

"Well, is he going to be?"

"No, we'll take him on to the Dentons if he can be moved again after he gets here."

But fate willed otherwise. When Doctor Dempsy arrived on the early train there were no conflicting opinions as to his condition; it was critical, and there would have to be an operation within twenty-four hours. Miss Maxwell brought the news to Peter along with the doctor's wish that his friend should be with him as long as the powers allowed.

"Does Leerie know?" asked Peter.

"She was present at the consultation."

"What did she say?"

"Nothing. But she looked very white and drawn. I'm afraid she hasn't slept much."

"Good Lord! you don't believe she really thinks Brainard will bungle!"

But Miss Maxwell cut him short. "This is no time to bother with futile suppositions. Please, Mr. Brooks! Remember that for all our sakes—Doctor Dempsy's most of all—this is the time to keep our nerve and think only one way." With a grave shake of the head she left him at the door of Doctor Dempsy's room.

To Peter the day crept on at a snail's pace; to Sheila it galloped. Peter saw her just once, when, at Doctor Dempsy's urgent wish, she came in for a moment between operations, muffled to the eyes in her gown and mask.

"Come here, child." The old doctor held out a commanding hand and drew the nurse close to the bed. "I've had something on my mind ever since I saw your face this morning. Might as well say it now before I forget it." He smiled up gently at the great, deep-gray eyes looking down wistfully at him. "I imagine that you two youngsters may be fretting some over to-morrow—seven A.M. Hey? Mean trick to saddle you with the responsibility of an old, worn-out hulk like mine, with the chances fifty-fifty on patching it up. What I wanted to say was that you mustn't take it too hard if I don't patch. 'Pon my soul I sha'n't mind for myself."

A voice called from the corridor outside, "Miss O'Leary, Doctor Brainard's waiting."

Doctor Dempsy gave the hand inside the rubber glove a tight squeeze. "Remember, Leerie, I know you'll keep the little old lantern burning for me as long as you can, and here's good luck, whatever happens."

She went without a word. Peter had become vastly absorbed at the window in watching Hennessy sweeping a gathering of leaves from the curb. When he finally came back to his chair by the bedside he flattered himself that his expression was beatifically cheerful and his voice perfectly steady.

As the day waned a storm gathered, and by nightfall the sanitarium and the surrounding country were in the grip of a full-fledged equinoctial. Doctor Dempsy was put to bed early, and Peter went back to his room in the main building to write himself into a state of temporary forgetfulness, if he could. He had tinkered with his pen, sharpened half a dozen pencils, and mussed up as many sheets of paper when a knock brought him to his feet. Sheila O'Leary stood at the door. Her lips were bravely trying to smile away the haggard lines of the face.

Unconsciously Peter's arms went out to her as he repeated that old cry of his in the days when he was a sufferer in the Surgical, "Why—why, it's Leerie!" and his love seemed to pound through every syllable.

For the flash of a second the eyes of the girl leaped to his in answer, but in another flash they seemed to have traveled miles away, looking back at him with the sadness of a lost angel. "Yes, it's Leerie again—come for help," she announced, tersely.

"All right." Peter tried to sound matter-of-fact.

"Don't ask questions; just do it. Will you?"

Peter nodded.

"You said once if you had to, you could drive through any storm, snow, hail, or rain, that you had ever seen. Yes? Then get your car and take Doctor Brainard out to-night. Take him anywhere, and keep him going till he's so tired he's ready to drop. Talk to him, tell him stories, don't let him talk about himself—or to-morrow. And bring him home when you think he can sleep."

"Yes. What are you going to do?"

"Sleep, I hope." She turned to go, but came back again and laid a cold hand in Peter's. "Thank you. Don't think I don't appreciate it."

"Wait a minute. As it happens, I haven't met Doctor Brainard, and there's a perfectly good chance he may not care about joy-riding in a young hurricane—even in my company," Peter ended ironically.

Leerie gave a little hollow laugh. "Oh, he'll go—don't worry. I'll bring him down and introduce him. Ready in ten minutes?" And this time she was gone.

Peter knew if he lived to the ripe old age of Solomon himself he should never forget the smallest detail of that night—Doctor Brainard's curt, almost surly greeting, the plunge into the car, and the start. After that Peter felt like a mythological being piloting the elements. He headed for a state road, and for miles, neither of them speaking, the car streaked over what might have been the surface of the river of Lethe, or the strata of mist lying above Niflheim, for all the feeling of reality and substance it gave. He had the eery sensation that he might be forced to keep on and on till the end of the world, like the Flying Dutchman. He wondered what sin of his own or some one's else he might be expiating. They passed no living or mechanical thing; they had the road, the night, the storm to themselves. They might have gone ten miles or thirty before Doctor Brainard broke the silence.

"Gad! but you can drive!"

"Thank you. Like it?"

"Not exactly. But it's better than thinking."

"Works the other way with me; this sets me thinking." A sudden, heavier gust sent the car skidding across the road, and Peter's attention went to his wheel. Righting it, he went on, "This is the second time in my life I've felt something controlling me that was stronger than my own will."

"Nasty feeling. Lucky man if you've only felt it twice. What was it the first time?"

"Fear. That's what brought me here."

Peter felt the eyes of the doctor studying him in the dark. "I heard about your case. It was Leerie brought you through, too, wasn't it?"

Quick as a flash Peter turned. For the instant he forgot they were speeding at a forbidden rate down slippery macadam in a tempest, with his hand as the only controlling force. He almost dropped his wheel. "Why '*too*'? Is she pulling you through something?"

He could hear a heavy intake of breath beside him. Unconsciously he knew that his companion was no longer sitting limp with relaxed muscles. He seemed to feel every nerve and fiber in the body of the surgeon growing tense, which made his careless, inconsequential tone sound the more strange when he finally spoke:

"That's an odd question to put to a doctor. I was referring to Leerie's cases. She's pulled through hundreds of patients, you know; she's famous for it."

"Yes, I know," answered Peter. His voice sounded just as careless, but the hands that gripped the wheel were as taut as steel.

They swept on for another half-hour, the silence broken by an occasional yawn from the surgeon. At last Peter slowed down and looked at his watch. "Eleven-thirty. If we turn now we'll make the San about one. How's that for bedtime?"

"Gad! I'm ready now," and the doctor yawned again.

Peter timed it to a nicety. It was five minutes past one as he dropped Doctor Brainard at the Surgical, where he roomed. He was just driving off when Miss Jacobs hurried out of the entrance.

"Oh, Mr. Brooks, wait a minute, please. Doctor Dempsy isn't resting very well, and Miss Maxwell left word that if he called for you, you could sit with him. We can't get him to sleep, and he does want you."

"All right. I'll leave the car and come back."

As Peter took his chair again by his friend's bedside his face was set to as strong a purpose as Sheila O'Leary's had shown that day in the sanitarium grounds. "Want me to talk, old man?" he asked, quietly. "Maybe I can yarn you into forty winks. Shall I try?"

"Wish you would. It's funny how a man can go through this with a thousand or so patients and it seems like an every-day affair, but when it's himself—well, there's the rub." And the doctor smiled a bit sheepishly at his own ungovernable nerves.

Peter gripped his hand understandingly. "I know. It's the difference between fiction and autobiography as far as it touches your own sense of reality. Well, to-night shall we try fiction? Ever since they pulled me through here, I've had my mind on a yarn with a sanitarium or hospital for a background and a doctor for a hero. All this atmosphere gets into your blood. It keeps you guessing until you have to spin a yarn and use up the material."

"Anything for copy, hey?" the doctor chuckled.

"That's about it. Well, my yarn runs about this way." With the skill of an artist and the sympathy of a humanist—and the suppressed excitement of one who has something at stake—Peter drew his two principal characters, the conscientious, sensitive doctor possessed with the constant fear of that hypothetical case he might lose some day, and the smooth, scheming man a few years his senior who wanted to get his fellow-practitioner out of the way and marry the girl they both loved. Peter made the girl as adorable as a man in love might picture her.

"For a sixpence I'd wager you had fallen in love yourself." Doctor Dempsy chuckled again. "I never before knew you to be so keen over feminine charms."

"Just more copy," and Peter went on with the tale. "Well, the young chap's horror and fear kept growing with each new case, and the other chap kept sneering and suggesting that his nerves weren't fit, and his hand wasn't steady, and he worked too slowly. He kept it up until he got what he wanted; the young chap bungled his operation and lost his case."

"Poor devil! I know just what kind of torment he lived through." Doctor Dempsy raised himself on an elbow and shook his head at Peter. "A case like that may be fiction to you, but it's fact to us in the profession. You have no idea how often a youngster's nerves fail him."

"Guess I'm getting the idea. But I need your help to finish the yarn. Of course the hospital couldn't bounce him for losing one case. They would have to prove first that he wasn't fit, wouldn't they?"

"They would have to make him out incompetent."

Peter nodded. Had there been more light in the room Doctor Dempsy might have been startled at the unprecedented expression of cunning that had crept into his friend's face. "I'm not up enough in medical matters to know what I could prove against the young chap to put him out. You'll have to help me. Just how could his rival oust him?"

"Accuse him of drugs," came the unhesitating answer. "That's the most plausible, and it's what plays havoc with young surgeons quicker than anything else. They feel their nerves going, and they take a hypodermic; it steadies them until—it gets them. If you can make your villain convince the staff that drugs are back of the lost case, you can get your poor devil of a surgeon permanently disposed of."

Peter let out a long-drawn breath. "Thank you, Doc. You've helped me out—considerably."

It does not in the least matter how Peter finished the tale. Before the inevitable conclusion Doctor Dempsy dropped off to sleep, and no one but Peter himself heard the final, "And they married and lived happy ever after. By Jupiter they did!"

He slipped softly out of the room and stood a moment in the corridor, wondering what he would do next. Sleep seemed unnecessary just then, as well as undesirable. And as he stood there, innocent of all intention of eavesdropping, he had that rare experience of hearing history repeat itself. From around the bend of the corridor, out of sight, came the low but distinct whisper of the night nurse's voice at the house 'phone.

"Miss Maxwell, Miss Maxwell, can you hear me? This is Miss Jacobs. Leerie went to Doctor Brainard's room a half-hour ago. She's still there.... All right." And then the soft click of the receiver dropping into place.

Peter stiffened; his hands clenched. His first impulse was to creep 'round and quietly choke the tattle-tale breath out of Miss Jacobs. He knew how the little green-eyed nurse was gloating over this second incrimination of Leerie. But there was something more compelling to do first, something that could not wait. He slipped 'round through the supply-room and down the back stairs. He reached the first floor of the Surgical just as the superintendent of nurses appeared in the entrance.

"You!" demanded Miss Maxwell.

"No one else," agreed Peter. "Suppose we go up together."

Peter could have almost laughed at the look of dumfounded amazement on the superintendent's face. "You mean—Why, that's impossible! It isn't your place—"

Peter cut her short. "Oh yes, it is. Remember the advice you gave me a few hours ago. I'm here to find out what's back of it all, and no one is going to stop me." His jaws snapped with an ominous finality.

Doctor Brainard opened to their knock, but he held the door so that barely a corner of the room was visible, and he blocked the entrance.

"Open it wider!" commanded Peter. "We've come to stay a few minutes and ask Miss O'Leary a few questions," and he thrust the surgeon quickly aside and flung wide the door.

Sheila was sitting by a reading-lamp, an open book on her lap. She looked as Peter had seen her in the early evening, only back of the tiredness and pallor was a strange look of peace. To Peter she seemed a crucified saint who had suddenly discovered that nail wounds were harmless. She smiled faintly at them both. "I'm sorry it's happened again, Miss Maxwell. If you'll just go away and try to forget about it until after the morning, I'll send in my resignation and leave as soon as you can fill my place. And can't we do it this time without any Board meeting? I'll promise never to come back."

"Then there are going to be no explanations this time—either?" There was pleading in the superintendent's voice, as well as infinite sadness.

The girl shook her head. "There's nothing to explain. I'm just here." She folded her hands quietly on her lap. "Won't you please go?"

"No, we won't!" Peter thundered it forth. Then he turned to the surgeon, and there was no pleading in his voice. "You cur! you cad! What have you got to say?"

Doctor Brainard jumped as if Peter had struck him; for the instant he seemed to find speech difficult. "Why—why, what do you mean? How dare you—"

"I dare you," and Peter shot out each word with the directness of a hand-grenade, "I dare you to stand up like a man and tell why Miss O'Leary came here to-night. You sneaked behind her silence three years ago; don't be a cursed coward and do it again."

The surgeon laughed a dry, unpleasant laugh. "It's easy to call another man names—but it doesn't mean anything. And what right have you to ask me to betray Miss O'Leary's silence?"

"Betray!" Peter fairly howled back the word at him. "Take off your coat. Take it off, or I'll rip it off. Now roll up your sleeves—no, your left. There, by Jupiter! Look, Miss Maxwell!"

Peter's demand was unnecessary. The eyes of the superintendent were already fixed on the manifold tiny blue discolorations in the surgeon's bare arm. "Cocaine." She almost whispered it under her breath, and then louder, "How long?"

"Four years, about." The surgeon's voice was quite toneless; he seemed to shrink and grow old while they watched him.

Miss Maxwell looked across at the girl, who was leaning forward, her face in her hands, crying softly. Her eyes were bitterly accusing, and there was abundant scorn in her voice when she spoke again to the surgeon. "So Leerie has been shielding you all along and helping you to fight it. How did she know?"

"I told her. I thought if some one with a courage and trust like hers knew about it it might pull me together. God! I wish I'd killed myself three years ago."

"Pity you didn't!" There was no mercy in Peter's voice. "But I suppose she wouldn't let you; I suppose she held you together then as she's trying to now. She's trying to save you for to-morrow—seven A.M.—and all the to-morrows coming after. I—I think I'm beginning to understand." His arms dropped dejectedly to his sides. For Peter there could be but one meaning to Sheila's sacrifice and struggle.

But Miss Maxwell was holding fast to her cross-examination. "And I suppose you promised Leerie three years ago if she'd keep silent you would fight it through and break the habit. And that's why you've let no one but Leerie and Miss Jacobs in the operating-room, so no one else would guess. Did Miss Jacobs find out three years ago?"

Doctor Brainard nodded.

Words failed the superintendent, but her expression boded ill for the little green-eyed nurse. "Well," she said, at length, "there's only one thing that matters right now—are you or are you not going to be in a fit condition to operate to-morrow?"

It was Leerie who answered. She was out of her chair at a bound and beside the surgeon, her hand on his arm. "He's going to operate; he's got to. There isn't another skilled hand like his nearer than the Dentons, so he's got to bring Doctor Dempsy through. Please, Miss Maxwell, leave him to me. I can manage. He's got four hours to sleep, and then I'll let him have enough cocaine to steady him. Won't you trust me?"

"It's about the only way now."

Peter left unnoticed. He realized, as he had realized in the sanitarium grounds that afternoon, that he counted about as much in this crisis as a part of the inanimate surroundings. Miss Maxwell joined him a moment later, looking outrageously relieved. She flashed Peter an apologetic smile.

"I know it's shameless of me to look glad when you look so miserable. But I can't help feeling that we are going to win. Leerie deserves it after what she's suffered for him. That man couldn't fail her, and her trust is bound to make good. Don't you see?"

Peter's shoulders gave an unconvincing shrug. "I hope so. He ought to—if he's half-way a man." He looked at his watch. "Almost morning now. Guess I'll pack my things and be ready to start as soon as I know Dempsy's all right."

Miss Maxwell held him back for an instant. "I know you're thinking that all's wrong with the world, but I know all's right. Go and pack if you must, but please stay in your room until I send you word. Promise?"

And not caring, Peter promised.

From seven o'clock on Peter paced the room among his packed luggage and counted the minutes. He wondered how long his patience would last and when his misery would stop growing. The burden of both had become unbearable. At eight-thirty a sharp knock sounded and he sprang to the door. On the threshold stood a nurse in surgical wrappings, with eyes that shone like a whole firmament of stars and a mouth that curved to the gentle demureness of a nun. Peter stood and stared at this unexpected apparition of the old Leerie.

"Well," said the apparition, smiling radiantly as of old, "I'm a messenger of glad tidings. Won't you ask me to come in?"

Peter flushed and drew her to a chair.

"Oh, it was a wonderful operation. It seemed almost like performing a miracle, and that blessed old doctor is coming out of the ether like a baby."

"Maybe it was a miracle—the miracle of a woman's trust."

A look of rare tenderness swept into the girl's face. "Thank you. I wonder if you know how often you say the kindest and most comforting thing." Then she sobered. "He's made a brave fight, and it wasn't easy to pull himself together, in the face of what he knew you were all thinking of him, and do such a tremendous piece of work. I want you to understand. He's a brilliant surgeon; it didn't seem right that he should be lost to himself and the profession. And the best of it is, he isn't going to be. The San is going to stand by him; every doctor on the staff is willing to help him. As soon as Doctor Jefferson is back, Doctor Brainard is to stop work until—until he's fit again. Isn't that splendid! Oh, I could sing! I keep saying over those great Hebrew words of comfort, 'Weeping may tarry through the night, but joy cometh in the morning.'"

"Yes," said Peter, dully. "I'm glad joy has come for you. May I wish you and Doctor Brainard all success and happiness?"

Sheila's eyes looked into Peter's with a sudden intensity. "You may—but not together. Have you actually been thinking that I loved Doctor Brainard?" A hint of the old bitterness crept into her voice. "I can pity a man like that, but love him—love weakness and selfishness—and the willingness to betray a woman's honor—no! Three years ago he killed whatever personal feeling I might have had for him, and he made me hate all men."

"And you're still hating them?" Peter held fast to his rising hopes while he hung eagerly on her answer.

"No. Ever since a fine, strong, unselfish man came into my life it has set me loving all mankind so scandalously that I'm afraid the only way to make me respectable is—for some man to marry me." Leerie's arms went out to Peter in complete surrender. "Oh, Peter—Peter—it's morning!"

But it was almost noon before Peter began to think intelligently again, and then he remembered something, something that ought to be done. "I think," he said, "I think we ought to go out and tell Hennessy and the swans; we sort of owe it to them."

And it all ended even as Peter had prophesied in his yarn by Doctor Dempsy's bedside.

Chapter V

THE LAST OF THE SURGICAL

THINGS have a way of beginning casually, so casually that you think they are bound to spin themselves out into airy nothings. The first inkling you have to the contrary is that headlong plunge into one of the big moments of your life, perhaps the biggest. But you never cease to wonder at the innocent, inconsequential way it began. These are the moments when you can picture Fate, sitting like an omnipotent operator before some giant switchboard, playing with signals and the like. I dare say he grins like a mischievous little boy who delights in turning things topsy-turvy whenever he has a chance.

Fate had been busy at this for some time when the sanitarium, quite oblivious of any signal connection, set itself to the glorious business of getting Sheila O'Leary married. Grief, despair, disappointment came often to the San, death not infrequently, but happiness rarely, and there had never before been such a joyous, personal happiness as this one. Small wonder that the San should gather it close to its heart and gloat over it! Was not Sheila one of its very own, born under its portals, trained in its school, placed above all its nurses, and loved beyond all else? And Peter Brooks. Had not the San given him his life and Sheila? It certainly was a time for rejoicing. As Hennessy had voiced it:

"Sure, half the weddin's ye go to ye sit miserable, thinkin' the man isn't good enough for the lass, or the lass is no mate for the man. But, glory be to Pether! here's a weddin' at last that God Almighty might be cryin' the banns for."

They were to be married within the month. Every one was agreed to this, from the superintendent down to Flanders, the bus-driver—yes, and even the lovers themselves. The San forgot its aches and sorrows in the excitement of planning an early summer wedding.

"We'll make the chapel look lovely," chirped the Reverend Mrs. Grumble, clasping and unclasping her hands in a fidget of anticipation. "There'll be enough roses and madonna lilies in the gardens to bank every pew and make an arch over the chancel."

"Well, if Leerie's married in the chapel, half of us can't get in." And Madam Courot shook her head in emphatic disapproval. "She'd better take the

Congregational church. That's the only place large enough to hold everybody who will want to come."

A mutinous murmur rose and circled the patients on the veranda. Not married at the San! It was unthinkable. So this point and the final date Sheila settled for them.

"We'll have the wedding in the gardens, save all the fuss and waste of picking the flowers, be ever so much prettier, and everybody and his neighbor can come."

When Hennessy heard of it he shirred his mouth into a pucker and whistled ecstatically. "'Tis like her, just! Married out-o'-doors wi' the growin' things to stand up wi' her and the blessed sun on her head. Faith, Hennessy will have to be scrubbin' up the swans an' puttin' white satin bows round their necks."

Sheila chose the hour before sunset on an early day of June, and the San speedily set itself to the task of praying off the rain and arranging the delightful details of attendants, refreshments, music, and all the other non-essentials of a successful wedding. Miss Maxwell, the superintendent of nurses, took the trousseau in hand and portioned out piles of napery and underwear to the eager hands of the nurses to embroider. The whole sanitarium was suddenly metamorphosed into a Dorcas Society; patients forgot to be querulous, and refused extra rubbings and all unnecessary tending, that more stitches might be taken in the twenty-four hours of the hospital day. A great rivalry sprang up between the day and night nurses as to which group would finish the most, and old Mr. Crotchets, the cynical bachelor with liver complaint and a supposedly atrophied heart, offered to the winning shift the biggest box of candy New York could put up.

Through the first days of her happiness Sheila walked like a lambent being of another world, whose radiance was almost blinding. Those who had known her best, who had felt her warmth and beauty in spite of that bitterness which had been her shield against the hurt she had battled with so long, looked upon her now with unfathomable wonder. And Peter, who had worshiped her from the moment she had taken his hand and led him back to the ways of health, watched her as the men of olden times must have watched the goddesses that occasionally graced their earth.

"Beloved, you're almost too wonderful for an every-day, Sunday-edition newspaper-man like me," Peter whispered to her in the hush of one twilight, as they sat together in the rest-house, watching Hennessy feed the swans.

"Every woman is, when the miracle of her life has been wrought for her. Man of mine," and Sheila reached out to Peter's ever waiting arms, "wouldn't God be niggardly not to let me seem beautiful to you now?"

Peter laughed softly. "If you're beautiful now, what will you be when—"

Sheila hushed him. "Listen, Peter, our happiness frightens me, it's so tremendous for just two people—almost more than our share of life. I know I seem foolish, but long ago I made up my mind I should have to do without love and all that goes with it, and now that it has come—sorrow, death, never frightened me, but this does."

"Glad I have the courage for two, then. Look here, Leerie, the more happiness we have the more we can spill over into other lives and the brighter you can burn your lamp for the ones in the dark. This old world needs all the happiness it can get now. So?"

Sheila smiled, satisfied. "You always understand. If I ever write out a prescription for love, I shall make understanding one-third of the dose. Let's go into partnership, Brooks and O'Leary, Distillers and Dispensers of Happiness."

"All right, but the firm's wrong. It's going to be Brooks and Brooks," and Peter kissed her.

"There is one thing," and Sheila gently disentangled herself. "There are days and days before the wedding, and if everybody thinks I am going to do nothing until then, everybody is very much mistaken. I'm going in this minute to sign up for my last case in the Surgical."

It must have been just at this moment that Fate turned on an arbitrary signal-light and changed a switch. I should like to think that back of his grin lurked a tiny shadow of contrition.

"And what am I going to do?" Peter called dolefully after her.

"Oh, I don't know. You might write an article on the dangers and uncertainties of marrying any woman in a profession." And she blew him a farewell kiss.

The train from the city, that night, brought a handful of patients, and one of these wore the uniform and insignia of a lieutenant of the Engineers. His mother came with him. She had been an old patient, and because of extraordinary circumstances—I use the government term—she had obtained his discharge from a military hospital and had brought him to the San to mend.

"The wounds are slow in closing, and there's some nervous trouble," Miss Maxwell explained to Sheila. "The boy's face is rather tragic. Will you take the case?"

She accepted with her usual curt nod and a hasty departure for her uniform. A half-hour later she was back in the Surgical, her fear as well as her happiness forgotten in the call of another human being in distress. The superintendent of nurses was right: the boy's face was tragic, and a frail little mother hovered over him as if she would breathe into his lungs the last breath from her own. She looked up wistfully, a little fearsomely, as Sheila entered; then a smile of thanksgiving swept her face like a flash of sunlight.

"Oh, I'm so glad! I remember you well. I hoped—but it hardly seemed possible—I didn't dare really to expect it. When I was here before, you were always so needed, and my boy—of course there is nothing serious— only—" and the shaking voice ended as incoherently as it had begun.

The nurse took the withered hands held out to her in her young, warm ones. In an instant she saw all that the little mother had been through—the renunciation months before when she had given her boy up to his country; the long, weary weeks of learning to do without him; the schooling it had taken to grow patient, waiting for the letters that came sparingly or not at all; and at last the news that he was at the front, under fire, when the papers published all the news there was to be told. Sheila saw it all, even to her blind, frantic groping for the God she had only half known and into whose hands she had never wholly given the keeping of her loved ones. And after that the cable and the waiting for what was left of her boy to come home to her. As she looked down at her, Sheila had the strange feeling that this frail little mother was dividing the care of her boy between God and herself, and she smiled unconsciously at this new partnership.

Gently she laid her hand on the lean, brown one resting on the coverlet; the boy opened his eyes. "It's going to be fine to have a soldier for a patient; I expect you know how to obey orders. You are our first, and we're going to make your getting well just the happiest time in all your life, the little mother and I."

The boy made no response. He looked at his mother as if he understood, and then with a groan of utter misery he turned away his head and closed his eyes again. "Ah-h-h!" thought Sheila, and a little later she drew the mother into the corridor beyond earshot.

"There's something ailing him besides wounds. What is it?"

"Clarisse." The promptness of the answer brought considerable relief to the nurse. It was easy to deal with the things one knew; it was the hidden things, tucked away in the corners of the subconscious mind or the super-sensitive soul, that never saw the light of open confession, that were the baffling obstacles to nursing. Sheila never dreaded what she knew.

"Well, what's the matter with Clarisse?" she asked, cheerfully.

The little mother hesitated. Evidently it was hard to put it into words. "They're engaged, she and Phil, and Phil doesn't want to see her, shrinks from the very thought of it. That's what's keeping him from getting better, I think. She's very young and oh, so pretty. They were both young when Phil went away—but Phil—" She stopped and passed a fluttering hand across her forehead; her lips quivered the barest bit. "Phil has come back so old. That's what war does for our boys; in just a few months it turns them into old men, the serious ones—and their eyes are older than any living person's I ever saw."

"And Clarisse is still young. I think I understand."

"That's why I brought him here. In the city there would have been no reason for her not coming to the hospital, but she couldn't come here unless we sent for her—could she?" Again the fluttering hand groped as if to untangle the complexity of thoughts and feelings in the poor confused head. "I write her letters. I make them just as pleasant as I can. I don't want to hurt her; she's so young."

Sheila nodded. "Does he love her?" That was the most important, for to Sheila love was the key that could spring the lock of every barrier.

"He did, and I think she loves him—I think—"

Sheila went back to her patient and began the welding of a comradeship that only such a woman can weld when her heart is full with love for another man. Day by day she made him talk more. He told her of his soldiering; apparently everything that had happened before held little or no place in his scheme of life, and he told it as simply and directly as if he had been a child. He made her see the months of training in camp, when he grew to know his company and feel for the first time what the brotherhood of arms meant. He told of the excitement of departure, the spiritual thrill of marching forth to war with the heart of a crusader in every boy's breast. His eyes shone when he spoke of their renunciation, of the glory of putting behind them home and love until the world should be made clean again and fit for happiness.

Sheila winced at this, but the boy did not notice; he was too absorbed in the things he had to tell.

He told of the days of waiting in France, with the battle-front before them like a mammoth drop-curtain, screening the biggest drama their lives would ever know. "There we were, marking time with the big guns, wondering if our turn would come next. That was a glorious feeling, worth all that came afterward—when the curtain went up for us."

He raised himself on an elbow and looked into Sheila's cool, gray eyes with eyes that burned of battle. "God! I can't tell you about it. There have been millions of war books written by men who have seen more than I have and who have the trick of words—and you've probably read them; you know. Only reading isn't seeing it; it isn't *living it*." He turned quickly, shooting out a hand and gripping hers hard. "Tell me; you've seen all sorts of operations—horrible ones, where they take out great pieces of malignant stuff that is eating the life out of a man. You've seen that?"

The nurse nodded.

"Did you forget it afterward, when the body was clean and whole again? Could you forget the thing that had been there? For that's war. That's what we're fighting, the thing that's eating into the heart of a decent, sound world, and since I've seen the horror of it I can't forget. I can't see the healing—yet."

"You will. Not at first, perhaps, but when you're stronger. That is one of God's blessed plans: He made beauty to be immortal and ugliness to die and be forgotten. And even the scars where ugliness was time whitens and obliterates. Give time its chance."

It was the next day that the boy spoke of Clarisse. "Will time make them all right, too? Leerie," he had picked up the nickname from the other nurses and appropriated it with all the ardent affection of worshiping youth, "we're miles—ages—apart. Can anything under God's canopy bring us together, I wonder?"

"Perhaps." Sheila smiled her old inscrutable smile. "Tell me more."

And so he told her of the girl who was so young, and oh, so pretty. It had all seemed right before he had gone to camp; it was the great love for him, something that had made his going seem the worthier. But at camp the distance between them had begun to widen, her letters had failed to bridge it, and through those letters he had discovered a new angle of her, an angle so acute that it had cut straight to the heart and destroyed all the love that had been there. At least that was what he thought.

"I knew she was young, of course, not much more than a child, and I knew she loved fun and good times, and all that, but—Why, she'd write about week-end parties, and how becoming her bathing-suit was, and what Tommy Flint said about her fox-trotting. Lord!" He writhed under the coverlet and ground his nails into his palms. "We marched through places where there wasn't a shred of anything left for anybody. We saw old women hanging on to broken platters and empty bird-cages because it was all they had left—home, children, everything gone. And on top of that would come a letter telling how much she'd spent on an evening gown, and how Bob Wylie took them out to Riverdale and blew in a hundred and twenty dollars on the day's trip. A hundred and twenty dollars! That would have bought a young ocean of milk over there for the refugee kids I saw starving."

He jerked himself up suddenly and sat huddled over, his eyes kindling with a vision of purging the world. Sheila knew it was useless to stop him, so she propped him up with pillows and let him go on.

"And that wasn't all. Between the lulls in the fighting they moved us along to a quiet sector, to freshen up, where we were so close to the German side that we could look into one of their captured villages. There we could see the French girls they'd carried off going out to work, saw them corralled at night like—" He broke off, hesitated, then went doggedly on. "With field-glasses we could see them plainly, the loads they had to lift and carry, the beatings they got, the look in their faces. Their shoulders were crooked, their backs bent from the long slaving. They were wraiths, most of them—and some with babies at their breasts. After I got back from seeing that, I found another letter from Clarisse. She said the girls just couldn't buckle down to much Red Cross work; it was so hard to do anything much in summer. They'd no sooner get started than some one would say tennis or a swim. *And I saw women dying over there—and bearing Boche babies!*"

All the agony of soul that youth can compass was poured forth in those last words. The boy leaned back on his pillows, weary unto death with the hopelessness of it all. So Sheila let him lie for a while before she answered him.

"Do the boys want their girls to know the full horror of it all? I thought that was one of the things you were fighting for, to keep as much of it away from them as you could."

The boy raised a hand in protest, but Sheila silenced him. "Wait a minute; it's my turn to talk now. I know what's in your mind. You think that Clarisse—and the girls like her—are showing unforgivable callousness and flippancy in the face of this world tragedy. Instead of becoming women as you have become men, they stay silly, unthinking, irresponsible creatures who dance and play and laugh while you fight and die. The contrast is too colossal; it all seems past remedy. Isn't that so? Well, there's another side, a side you haven't thought of. The girls are giving you up. The little they know of life, as it is now, looks very overwhelming to them. Perhaps it frightens them. And what do frightened children do in the dark?"

The boy did not try to answer; he waited, tensely eager.

"Why, they sing; they laugh little short-breathed laughs; they tell stories to themselves of nonsensical things to reassure them. All the time they are trying not to think of what terrors the dark may hold; they are trying not to cry out for some one to come and sit with them. Some of our girls are doing a tremendous work. They meet trains at all hours of the day or night and feed the boys before they sail; they wait all day in the canteens until they're ready to drop; they put in a lot more time, making comfort-kits, knitting, and rolling bandages, than they ever own to. And suppose they don't grow dreadfully serious; isn't it better that way? The girls are doing their bit as fast as they are learning how. It isn't fair of the boys to judge them too soon. It isn't fair of you to judge your Clarisse without giving her a chance."

"You didn't read those letters."

"Letters! Most of us, when we write, keep back the things that really matter and skim off the surface of our lives to tell about. There may not be the sixteenth part of your girl in those letters."

The boy's lips tightened stubbornly. "It wasn't just one—it was all of them. Anyhow, I haven't the nerve or the heart to find out."

Again Sheila let the silence fall between them. When she spoke, her voice was very tender. "Tell me, boy, what made you love her?"

He smiled sheepishly. "Oh, I don't know. She was always a good sport, never got grumpy over things that happened, never got cold feet, either. She had a way of teasing you to do what she wanted, would do anything to get her way; and then she'd turn about so quickly and give you your way, after all—just make you take it. And she'd be so awfully sweet about it, too. And she'd always play fair, and she had a way of making you feel the best ever. Oh, I don't know—" The boy looked about him helplessly. "They sound awfully foolish reasons for loving a girl."

Sheila's face had become suddenly radiant; her eyes sparkled like rushlights in a wind. They actually startled the boy so that he straightened up in bed again and gripped her hand. "I say, Leerie, what is it? I never saw you look like this before. You're—Are you in love?"

"With one of the finest men God ever made. He's so fine that he trusted me through a terrible bungle—believed in the real woman in me when I would have denied it. That's what a man's love can do for a woman sometimes, keep her true to the best in her."

That night, after many fluttering protests, the little mother wrote a letter to Clarisse. It was dictated by Sheila and posted by her, and it contained little information except what might have been extracted from a non-committal railroad guide. It did mention at the last, however, that Phil was slowly gaining.

With this off her mind, Sheila went to find Peter. She had characteristically neglected him since she had been on the case, and as characteristically he made no protest. Instead he met her with that quick understanding that she had claimed as one of love's ingredients. He looked her over well and proudly, then tapped his head significantly.

"I see, there's more to this soldier-boy case than just wounds. Want me to run you down the boulevard while you work it out?"

"Thank God for a man!" breathed Sheila, and then aloud: "No, it's worked out. But you might run me down, just the same."

"Feels almost like frost to-night," said Peter as he put the car into first. "Do you think it will hold pleasant enough for—"

"For what?" Sheila's tone sounded blank.

Peter chuckled. "For the gardens and the old ladies, of course. Have you by any chance forgotten that there's going to be a wedding in four days?"

"Saturday, Sunday, Monday, Tuesday—" counted Sheila. "Why, so it is!" Then she echoed Peter's chuckle, "Oh yes, there's going to be a wedding, a beautiful wedding in four days."

A strange little twinge took Peter's heart there in the dark at the queer, impersonal note in what she had said. What did it mean?

Sheila gave the girl twenty-four hours to reach the San after receiving the letter; she came in eighteen, and the nurse rejoiced at this good omen. She had delegated Peter to meet all trains that day, take the girl to her room, send for her at once, and tell nobody. Peter obeyed, and early in the afternoon Sheila looked up from her reading to the boy to see Peter standing in the doorway, the message on his lips.

"Baggage delivered," was Peter's announcement.

"Thank you. I'll come in a minute and see if my key fits." She hunted up the little mother, left her in charge, and hurried over to the nurses' home.

There in the big living-hall, perched in a wicker chair under the poster of Old King Cole, Sheila found the girl, who was young and oh, so pretty. She looked about as capable of taking a plunge into the grim depths of life and coming out safely as a toy Pom of weathering the waters of the Devil's Hole. "How shall I ever push her in?" thought Sheila as she held out her hand in greeting.

Clarisse took it with all the hectic impulsiveness of youth. "You're his nurse. Isn't it great his coming back this way? All our set is engaged—or about to be—but I'm the only one that's got her man back with battle scars all over him. Makes me feel like a story-book heroine."

Sheila O'Leary didn't know whether she wanted to laugh or cry. She ended by doing what probably surprised her more than it did the girl. She sat down in the wicker chair herself and gathered the girl into her lap. "Oh, you blessed, blessed baby!" she crooned softly.

The girl pouted adorably. It was very evident that she liked to be petted, coaxed, and spoiled. If there was a woman slumbering under all this dimpling, infantile charm, she was quite indiscernible to the woman who held her.

Slowly she bent over the girl and let her face show all the delight she could feel in her prettiness and baby ways. There must be sympathy between them or her task would be hopeless. "There, let me untie that bewitching bonnet of yours and take off your gloves. We have a lot to tell each other before you see your soldier."

"But Phil—won't he be waiting, wondering why I don't come? Oh, I'm just crazy to see him!"

"He doesn't know you're here yet."

"Oh!" The smooth, white forehead did its utmost to manage a frown. "Why, didn't he send for me?"

"No."

"Who did? His mother wrote."

"I sent."

The round, childish eyes filled with apprehension; she wrenched herself free of Sheila's arms. "He isn't going to—The letter said—?"

"He's better. Sit down, dear. That's what we have to talk over. His body is mending fast, but his mind—well, his mind has been taken prisoner."

Clarisse tossed an adorable crown of golden curls. "I don't understand."

"Didn't expect you to, at first. It's this way. He's been through some very big, very terrible experiences, and he can't forget them. He isn't the boy you used to play with, the boy who was happy just having a good time. He's grown very serious. That's what experience is likely to do for us all in time, but with him it's come all in a heap. When that happens you can't go back and be happy in the old way. Do you see?"

"Go on."

"He's bound fast and walled about with the memories of what he has been through—killing human beings, watching his comrades die, seeing what the Germans have done. For the moment it has made him forget that the sun shines and birds sing and the world is a place to be glad in. The bright colors have faded out of life for him; everything looks gray and somber."

"Gee! and how he used to like a good cabaret with a jazz band!" The girl whispered it, and there was awe in her voice. "And colors! I had to wear the gayest things I had, to please him."

"Yes, I know. And he'll like them best again, some day. Just be patient, dear. And the waiting won't be hard, you'll have so much to do for him. You'll have to be bringing the sunshine back, making him listen to the bird-songs, teaching him how to be glad, to love doing all the happy, foolish boy-things he used to like."

"I see—I can." The girl's voice was breathless.

"I'm sure you can." Sheila tried to put conviction into her words. "At first you may find it a little hard. It means—"

"Yes?"

"It means creeping into his prison with him, so gently, so lovingly, and staying close beside him while you cut the memory-cords one by one. Could you do that?"

The girl sprang past Sheila toward the door. "Come! What are we waiting for?"

"But he doesn't know you are here yet," parried the nurse.

"Let's go and tell him, then. He always adored surprises." The dimples in her cheeks danced in anticipation while she took Sheila's hand and tried to drag her nearer the door. But at the threshold something in the woman's face stopped her. She hesitated. "Maybe—maybe he doesn't like surprises any more." Again the impulsive hands were thrust into the nurse's. "Tell me, tell me honestly—You said you sent for me. Was it—Didn't he want me—to come?"

And Sheila, remembering what the boy had loved about her, gave her back the truth: "No, he has grown afraid of you. That's another thing you will have to bring back to him with the songs and the sunlight—his love for you."

Her hand was flung aside and the girl flew past her, back to the wicker chair under Old King Cole. Burying her head in her arms, she burst into uncontrollable sobs, while Sheila stood motionless in the doorway and waited. She must have waited an hour before the girl raised her eyes, wet as her own. For Sheila knew that a woman's soul was being born into the world, and none understood better than she what the agony of travail meant to the child who was giving it birth.

"Come," said Sheila, gently.

The girl rose uncertainly; all the divine assurance of youth was gone. "I think I see," she began unsteadily. "I think I can."

"I know you can." And this time there was no doubt in Sheila's heart.

She saw to it that the little mother had been called away before they reached the Surgical, so that the room was empty except for the occupant of the cot. "Hello, boy!" she called, triumphantly, from the doorway. "I have brought you the best present a soldier ever had," and she pushed Clarisse into the room and closed the door.

For a moment those two young creatures looked at each other, overcome with confusion and the self-consciousness of their own great change.

The boy spoke first. "Clare!"

"Phil!" It came in a breathless little cry, like a bird's answer to its mate. Then the girl followed. Across the room she flew, to the bed, and down on her knees, hiding her face deep in the folds of coverlet and hospital shirt. Words came forth chokingly at last, like bubbles of air rising slowly to the surface.

"Those letters—those awful letters! Just foolish things that didn't matter. One of the boys at the canteen—I used to wait on the table and make believe every soldier I served was mine, and I always wore my prettiest clothes—he said—the boy—that over there they didn't want anything but light stuff—those were his words—said a chap couldn't stand hearing that his girl was lonely.... He said to cut out all the blue funks and the worries; the light stuff helped to steady a chap's nerve. So I—"

And then the boy lied like a soldier. "Don't, Clare darling. I knew all along you were playing off like a good sport. And it helped a lot. Gee! how it helped!"

When Sheila looked in, hours later, the girl was still by the bed, her cheek on the pillow beside the boy's.

It was a strangely illusive Leerie that met Peter that night in the rest-house after the ailing part of the San had been put safely to bed. Her eyes seemed to transcend the stars, and her face might have served for a young neophyte. As Peter saw, for the first time he glimpsed the signal Fate had been playing with so many days.

"What's happened? Anything wrong with those cubs?"

"Nothing. They're as right as right can be." Then with the old directness Sheila plunged headlong into the thing she knew must be done. "Man of mine, I'm going to hurt you. Can you forgive and still understand?"

"I can try." Peter did his best to keep his voice from sounding too heavy, for a fear was gripping at his heart, and his eyes sought Sheila's face, pleading as he would never have let his lips plead.

Sheila covered her eyes. She didn't want to see. It was too reminiscent of the little boy lying awake in a dark attic, afraid of sleep. "We have both done without happiness so long, don't you think we can do without it a little longer?"

"I suppose so—if we must." Peter's voice was very dull. "But why? I've always had an idea that happiness was something like opportunity; it had to be snatched and held fast when it came your way, or you might never have another chance at it." Had Sheila brought him to the gates of Paradise only to bar them against his entering? he wondered.

The woman who loved him understood and laid her hand on his breast as if she would stay the hurt there if she could. "It may make it easier if you know that the giving up is going to be hard for me, too. I've thought about that home of ours so long that I've begun to see it and all that goes with it. I even stumble upon it in my dreams. It's always at the end of a long, tired road, going uphill. If I thought I should have to give it up, I wouldn't have the courage to do what I'm going to now."

She sat down on the bench, laid her arms over the sill of the rustic window, and looked toward the pond. The night was very still; the blurred outlines of the swans, huddled against the bank, were the only signs of life. When she spoke it was almost to herself.

"When they sent me away from the San three years ago I thought I could never bear it—to go away alone, that way, disgraced, to begin work over again in a strange place, among strange people. But I had to do it, just as I have to do this." She straightened and faced Peter. Her voice changed; it belonged to the curt, determined Sheila.

"I'm going across, to nurse the boys over there. The boy over in the Surgical pointed the way for me. There's a big thing going on in the world—something almost as big as the war—it's the business of getting the boys ready for life after their share in the war is over, and I don't mean just nursing their bodies back to health. Everything is changed for them; they've got new standards, new interests, new hearts, new souls, and we women have got to keep pace with them. And we mustn't fail them—don't you see that? Oh, I know I have no place of my own in the war: you are safe, and I have no brothers. But I'm a woman—a nurse, thank God! And I'm free to go for the mothers and sweethearts who can't. Don't you understand?"

And Peter answered from an overwhelmingly full and troubled heart, "Oh yes, I understand."

"I knew you would." Sheila raised starry eyes to the man who had never failed her. "Those boys will need all the sympathy, all the wholesome tenderness we can send across to them, and they'll need our hands at their backs until they get their foothold again. I've served my apprenticeship at that so long I can do it."

Peter gathered her close in his arms. "God and I know how well."

It was not until they were leaving the gardens that Peter asked the question that had been in his mind all through the evening. "What about the wedding? I suppose you're not going to marry me, now."

"Can't. Haven't the courage. Man of mine, don't you know that after I once belonged to you I couldn't leave you? I've only had sips of happiness so far. If I once drained the cup, only God's hand could take it from me."

"And the wedding? The old San's just set its heart on that wedding."

The radiant smile crept back to Sheila's lips. Even in the dark Peter could tell that the old luminous Leerie was beside him once more. "Why, that's one of the nicest parts of it all. We're going to pass our wedding on to those children—make them a sort of wedding-present of it. Won't that be splendid?"

"Oh yes," said Peter, without enthusiasm. "Does it suit them?"

"They don't know yet. Guess I'd better go and tell them."

It is doubtful if anybody but Sheila O'Leary could have managed such an affair and left every one reasonably happy over it—two of them unreasonably so. She accepted the wedding collation bestowed by the wealthy old ladies of the sanitarium and passed it over to the boy and his betrothed as if it had been as trivial a gift as an ice-cream cone. In a like manner she passed on the trousseau, kissed all the nurses rapturously for their work, and piled it all into Clarisse's arms with the remark that it was lucky they were so nearly of a size. When she brought the wedding-dress she kissed her, too, and said that she was going to make the prettiest picture in it that the San or the soldier had seen in years. She placated the management; she wheedled Miss Maxwell into a good humor; she even coaxed Doctor Fuller into giving away the bride. Only Hennessy refused to be propitiated.

"Are ye thinkin' of givin' Mr. Brooks away with everythin' else?" he asked, scornfully; and then, his indignation rising to a white wrath, he shouted, "I'll not put bows on the swans, an' I'll not come to any second-hand weddin'."

But he did come, and held with Flanders the satin ribbons they had promised to hold for Sheila. And the wedding became one of the greenest of all the memories that had gone down on the San books.

As the sun clipped the far-away hills the boy was wheeled down the paths to where the gold and white of early roses were massed in summer splendor. Then came the girl with Sheila at her side; the girl had begged too hard to be refused. But Sheila's face was as white as it had been the day they operated on Doctor Dempsy, and only Peter guessed what it cost her to stand with the bride. To Peter's care had been intrusted the little mother, and he let her weep continually on his shoulder in between the laughs he kept bringing to her lips.

And it all ended merrily. Sheila saw to that. But perhaps the thing that gave her the keenest pleasure was wheedling out of Mr. Crotchets his bungalow that stood on the slopes beyond the golf-links for a honeymoon.

"They'll have all the quiet they want and the care he still needs," she told Peter when they were alone. "And nobody but the nurse in charge knows about it—yet." Then seeing the great longing in Peter's eyes, she drew him away from the crowd. "Listen, man of mine! I have the feeling that when we are married there will be no wedding, just you and I and the preacher. And in my heart I like it better that way."

"So do I," agreed Peter.

"I'm leaving—train to-night," Sheila hurried on. "No use putting it off; better sail as soon as the passport's ready. There's just one thing more I want to say before I leave you."

Then Peter chuckled for the first time that day. "You can say it, of course, but if you think you're going to leave me behind, you're mistaken. I wired the chief the day you told me. They need another correspondent over there. When it comes to passports there is some advantage in not being a husband, after all. Well—are you glad?"

When Hennessy came upon them, a few minutes later, they looked so supremely happy and oblivious of the rest of the world that he was forced to stop. "Sure, ye might be the bride an' groom, afther all, by the looks of ye. What's come over ye all of a sudden?" And when Peter told him, and they both put their hands in Hennessy's in final parting, he shirred his lips and whistled forth evidence of a satisfied emotion to which he added a word of warning to Peter:

"I'm not envyin' ye, just the same, Mr. Brooks. Afore ye get her home again ye'll find the Irish say right, 'A woman's more throuble to look afther than a thorn in the foot or a goat fetched back from the fair!'"

Chapter VI

MONSIEUR SATAN

THERE had been nothing, perhaps, more radically changed by the rigors of war than Atlantic transportation. The thrills of pleasure and romance that attended the tourist in the days before the war had deepened to thrills of another timbre, while romance had become more epic than idyllic. The happy phrase of "going abroad" had given place to "going over" or "going across"; such a trifling difference in words, but the accompaniment comes in quite another key. It was no longer shouted in a care-free, happy-go-lucky fashion; it may have had a ring of suppressed exultation; but it was sure to be whispered with a quick intake of breath, and so often it came through teeth that were clenched.

The piers had changed their gala attire. The departure from this country for another was no longer a matter of mere rejoicing and congratulatory leave-taking. The gangways no longer swarmed with friends shouting, "Bon voyage!" There was no free voicing of anticipation, no effervescing of good humor. The Spirit of Adventure was there, but he had changed his costume and his make-up. So had the good ships. Their black paint and white trimmings were gone; gone were the gay red funnels; and in their stead were massed the grays and blues, the greens and blacks of camouflage. The piers were deserted. A thin stream of travelers sifted in; there were a few officials and deckhands; and far outside, beyond hail of ship or sea or traveler, in a barbed-wire inclosure, guarded by military police, stood a few scattered, silent figures. They were the remnants war had left of the once-upon-a-time jocose band of waving, shouting friends.

All this Sheila O'Leary felt as she stood on the upper deck of a French liner with Peter Brooks and watched their fellow-passengers board the ship. She was tingling from head to foot with almost as many emotions as there are ganglia in the nervous system. It was as if she had suddenly claimed the world for a patient and had laid fingers to its pulse for the first time. Eagerly, impatiently, she was waiting to count each successive beat until she should be able to read into the throbbing rhythm of it all a meaning for herself.

As Sheila thought in terms of her work, so Peter thought in terms of his. It was all copy to him. Each group that followed another up the gangway carried the promise of a story to Peter. There were Red Cross nurses, canteen workers, a college unit for reconstruction work, a hospital unit, scores of detached American officers going over for the first time, scores of French and British returning, a few foreigners getting back to their respective countries, and hosts of non-descripts whose civilian clothes gave no hint of their missions. Last of all came a sudden, swift influx of celestial blue.

Peter smiled at them with anticipation, "Look, Leerie, the Blue Devils of France! There ought to be the making of a good yarn."

But Sheila barely heard. The mass had captured her imagination on the instant with a dramatic intensity too overpowering to be denied. Unconsciously she smiled. They were going back to fight again—to be wounded. Who knew—in a month she might be nursing some of them. The Blue Devils had reached the gangway; they were just below them when one looked up. Black eyes as unfathomable as forest pools looked into Sheila's quiet gray ones. For a moment there was almost a greeting flashed between them; as if they recognized something common to them both that lay in the past or the future. It was one of those gossamer threads of fate that a few glimpse rarely in their lives.

Peter saw, and was on the point of giving tongue to his astonishment when a voice from behind interrupted them: "The ship sails at ten; it lacks thirty seconds of that. There is the typical instance of the way these Devils obey their orders. Is it not so?"

The voice savored of France. Sheila and Peter turned together to find a little man, with a small, pleasant face, topped with shaggy brown hair, and dabs of mustache and beard placed like a colon under his nose. His shrug was the conclusive evidence of his nationality.

"Well, thirty seconds is enough," laughed Sheila. "Time is as precious as food, gold, or gunpowder these days. Why waste it?"

"And men," supplemented the little man. "Perhaps, mad'moiselle already knows Bertrand Fauchet, the young captain who passed below?"

Sheila shook her head.

The little man rubbed his hands together in keen enjoyment. "Ah, there is a man; but they are all men. The Boches have named them well. They fight like demons, then they rest and play like children until their turn comes to fight again. And Fauchet—he is a devil of a devil, possessed of a thousand lives. Mad'moiselle would adore him."

Sheila's demure chin tilted mutinously, "But I don't like devils, even blue ones."

"Ah, you do not understand. C'est la guerre. We must lock away in our hearts all the pity, all the tenderness, as we hide our jewels and our treasures and mask our cathedrals. If we did not they would all be destroyed and we would go quite mad." He smiled whimsically at Sheila, as one smiles at a child who fails to comprehend. "Wait—wait till mad'moiselle sees France. Then—" He finished with a shrug and left them.

They were in midstream when they saw the little man again. He came hurrying toward them with both hands outstretched to Peter. "It is Mr. Brooks. I did not know when I was speaking with you and mad'moiselle before. They told me at the office of your paper that you would be sailing to-day. May I present Jacques Marchand of the *Figaro*, a fellow-journalist?" and he made a profound bow which included Sheila.

Peter introduced the girl beside him and the little man looked at her with whetted interest and a twinkle of suppressed humor. "You women of America, you come like battalions of good angels to nurse our devils. Eh bien, before the sun goes down you shall meet your first one. Au 'voir till then."

They were in the stern, watching the last of the sun in their wake as it turned myriads of whirring wings to iridescent gold, when the little man found them again. This time he was not alone. Close upon his heels came the captain of the Blue Devils; and again the black eyes met Sheila's when they were still a man's length apart.

"Mad'moiselle," said Jacques Marchand, "I have brought, as I promised—Monsieur Satan—Mad'moiselle O'Leary. Look him well over; you will see he has not the horns or cloven feet, nevertheless—mais, voilà."

The captain was blushing like a very bashful little boy; he was smiling as naïvely as an infant. Sheila guessed at his age and placed it not far from twenty. Who had ever conceived of a boy-Mephistopheles? It was absurd. A genuine diabolical personage had no right to a pre-middle age; for him all years prior to forty should not exist. And here was undeniably a boy, whose very bashfulness and naïveté bore witness that he had not entirely grown up. So Sheila smiled back upon him with the frankness and abandon one feels so safe in bestowing upon youth.

"This paper-man, he likes to be what you call funny. It pays him well, and he must keep, what you say, his feet in. But I do not like always his little jokes. I will make a new introduce so. Bertrand Fauchet, capitaine Chasseurs Alpins, very much at your service, ma'am'selle." The soldier bowed with solemnity. It was evident he felt his dignity had been trampled on and resented it.

The little man of the *Figaro* wagged a forefinger at him. "Ah, tata, garçon. Remember, I am your godfather in the battalion. It is I that give you the name. Three years ago in the Café des Alcazar I call you Monsieur Satan, and it stick. You cannot rub it off; you cannot make France forget it; and when you come back so fierce—so terrific from the fighting at Troyes where you get the Croix de Guerre it is not for Capitaine Fauchet the men shout—non. It is for Monsieur Satan they shout, for the devil of a Blue Devil. Eh, mon ami?" And he laid a loving arm across the other's shoulder.

During the crossing the four met often; the journalist always kindly and loquacious, Monsieur Satan always shy. Sometimes he joined Sheila alone for an after-dinner promenade. It was always at that hour when the day was fading into a luminous twilight that told of stars to come, and they tramped the decks in a strange, companionable silence. It was plain that Monsieur Satan did not wish to talk, and Sheila gave him freely the silence he craved. Once he stopped and looked over the railing, hard at the sea horizon.

"Did you ever think, ma'am'selle," he said, softly, "how the great ocean shows nothing of the war? The underneath may be choked with sunken ships, the murdered ships, but the ocean has no scars. It is not like our sorrowful France—all scars. So—I find it good to look at this and forget. Perhaps, some day, a peace like this will come to the heart of Bertrand Fauchet. Qui savez?"

And another time, when he was wishing her good night, he added: "Dormez bien—sans songes, ma'am'selle. The dreams, they are bad."

But generally he left her with just a pressure of the hand and an "*Au 'voir.*" And yet there was always in his voice a suppressed gratitude as for a gift.

When Peter was alone with him he tried to draw him out and got nothing for his pains. The story he had scented on their day of embarkation had undoubtedly left no trail. When he aired his disappointment good-naturedly to Sheila she only laughed at him.

"If you want a story go to some of the other devils; we'll never know more of Monsieur Satan till Fate turns interlocutor."

"Well, he's certainly the most slumbering devil I ever saw. If that's the worst French soil can propagate, it's hard to believe the Germans they tackle get much of an inferno."

In spite of his skepticism, however, Peter had an unexpected glimpse into that inferno the day before they landed. For thirty-six hours they had been running through the danger zone with life-boats loose on their davits, life-belts ready for adjustment, and nerves tense. Then the tension had suddenly relaxed, everybody talked with everybody else, displaying a lack of restraint that bordered on intimacy. Peter and Sheila were strolling an almost deserted deck toward a group amidships. As they neared it they saw it was dominated by two principal figures—one a professional philanthropist with more sentiment than judgment, and the other Monsieur Satan. The philanthropist was talking in what Peter termed an "open-throttle voice."

"But you don't mean you would ever harm a defenseless prisoner, Captain Fauchet? Of course you would never allow your men to kill a fallen enemy or one supplicating mercy."

"Supplicating mercy—bah!" The mouth that could smile so boyishly had a diabolical twist, the eyes blazed like hell-fires, as Peter said afterward. "There is only the one Boche that is safe, madame—the dead Boche. When we find them wriggling I teach my men to make them safe—quickly!" The lips smiled sardonically. Monsieur Satan was a boy no longer; in some inexplicable fashion he had come into full possession of that Mephistophelian middle-age.

But the lady philanthropist had neither the eyes to see nor the intelligence to understand. Instead she clumsily parried with invisible forces. "Of course you don't mean that, Captain Fauchet. You are just making believe you are a wicked man. I believe you are trying to stuff me, as our American slang puts it. Now if a wounded German came running toward you crying Kamerad—"

"Sacrebleu! Oui, madame, once I listen to that Kamerad. But now—jamais! When they call it with their lying tongues I shout them back 'Kamerad to hell!' and I zigeuille." The right hand made a swift, subtle twist with a deep thrust. It took little imagination to guess what it was supposed to be holding. For a second Monsieur Satan's eyes still continued to blaze at the woman before him; then he tossed back his head, plunged through the crowd, and was gone.

"A devil of a Blue Devil," quoted Peter under his breath. "Our friend, Monsieur Marchand, was not indulging in hyperbole after all."

Sheila watched him go and said nothing.

That twilight, when Monsieur Satan joined her, he looked as harmless as ever, only a trifle more bashful. "Perhaps ma'am'selle will care no longer to promenade with the wicked man. N'est ce pas?"

"A brave man," corrected Sheila, and she looked straight into the black eyes. "A brave man who has given himself body and soul to France."

"Body and soul. Oui, ma'am'selle. But listen—there is something—" His face changed in a breath, the eyes were blazing again, the mouth had turned as sinister as his *nom de guerre* signified. But something in Sheila's eyes checked him. He put out a hand unconsciously and laid it on her as though to steady himself. "Non, ma'am'selle. One need not tell everything. You will see enough—enough."

When they landed, his good-bys to her were curiously brief. He held her hand a second as if he would have said a great deal; then with a quick "*Au 'voir*" he flung it from him and was down the gangway. But with Peter it was different. He found him alone and vouchsafed him for the first time what might have been called conversation.

"I do not know until yesterday that you were betrothed to Ma'am'selle O'Leary. That is so?"

Peter nodded.

"You have been generous, monsieur. I wish to thank you."

Peter held out his hand. "Oh, that's all right. American men aren't given to being jealous, as a rule. Besides, Miss O'Leary is the sort one has no right to be selfish with. I guess you understand?"

"Oui, monsieur. She belongs a little to every one, man or child, who needs the sympathy, the kind word, the loving heart. Moi, I comprehend. Some time, perhaps, I render back the service. Then you can trust me; the honor of Bertrand Fauchet can be trusted with women. Adieu, monsieur."

By dawn the next day the passengers of the liner were scattering to the far corners of the fighting-front. Jacques Marchand had gone, *via* the office of the *Figaro*, to Flanders. Monsieur Satan had been despatched to relieve another captain of the Chasseurs Alpins with French outposts along the Oise. Peter had received his war permits to join the A. E. F. in action and Sheila had received her appointment to an evacuation hospital near the front. Her parting with Peter was over before either of them had time to realize it. Her train left the Gare du Nord before his. They had very little to say, these two who had claimed each other out of all the world and now were putting aside their personal happiness that they might give their service where it was so really needed. There were no whimperings of heart, no conscious self-righteousness; only a great gladness that hard work lay before them and that they understood each other.

"Good-by, man o' mine. Whatever happens, remember I am yours for always, and death doesn't count," and Sheila laid her lips to Peter's in final pledge.

"I know," said Peter. "That's what makes all this so absurdly easy. And, sweetheart, you are to remember this, never put any thought of me before what you feel you have got to do. Don't bungle your instincts. I'd swear by them next to God's own."

And so they went their separate ways.

There was no apprenticeship for Sheila in the hospital whither she was sent. The chief of the surgical staff gave a cursory glance over the letter she had brought from the San, signed by the three leading surgeons in that state; then he looked hard at her.

"Hm ... m! And strong into the bargain. You're a godsend, Miss O'Leary."

Before the day had gone she was in charge of one of the operating-rooms; by midnight they had fifty-three major operations. And the days that followed were much the same; they passed more like dreams than realities. There were a few sane, clear moments when Sheila realized that the sky was very blue or leaden gray; that the sun shone or did not shine, that the wards were cheery places and that all about her were faces consecrated to unselfish work or to patient suffering. These were the times when she could stop for a chat with the boys or write letters home for them. But for the most part she was being hurled through a maelstrom of operations and dressings with just enough time between to snatch her share of food and sleep. Her enthusiasm was unbounded for the marvelous efficiency of it all. She could never have believed that so many delicate operations could have been done in so few hours, that wounds could heal with such rapidity, that nerves could rebound and hearts come sturdily through to go about their business of keeping their owners alive. And every boy brought to her room was a fighting chance; but the fight was up to her and the surgeons, and they fought as archangels might to restore a new heaven on a befouled earth. Life had always seemed full and worth while to her. Now it seemed a super-life, shorn of everything petty and futile.

"War may be hell; very likely it is for those who make it; but for us who do the patching afterward it's like the Day of Creation. I feel as if I'd put new souls into mended bodies." And the gruff, overtired chief who heard her smiled and mumbled to himself, "Those of us who survive will all have new souls; old ones have atrophied and dropped off."

Fall was slow in coming. Instead of settling down to trench hibernating as had been the custom for three years, the Entente kept to its periodic attacks, pushing the enemy back farther and still a little farther, so that trenches were no longer the permanent abiding-places they had been in the past. Just as every one was prophesying the numbing of hostilities until spring, the rumor spread of Foch's final drive. On the heels of the rumor came the drive itself. Hospitals were taxed to their utmost; surgeons and nurses worked for days with a maximum of four hours' sleep a night. In

Sheila's hospital Anzacs, Territorials, poilus, Americans, Tommies, and Zouaves poured in indiscriminately. Mattresses covered every square inch on the floor and canvas was stretched in the yard over many more. The number of operating-tables gave out at the beginning and they used stretchers, boards—anything that could hold a wounded man.

"It's our last pull," said the doctors. "If we can keep going three—four more days, we'll have as many months to get back some of our wind."

"Of course we'll keep going," said the nurses. And they slept in their clothes for those days and did dressings in their sleep.

When it was over and they had settled down to what was near-routine again they began to sort out the minor cases and pass on the convalescents. Sheila, who had slept on the threshold of her room for weeks, was dragged forth by the chief to make the rounds with him and dispose of the negligible cases. It was in the last ward that she came upon Monsieur Satan.

From across the room she was conscious of the change in him. He was not much hurt—an exploding shell had damaged one foot and his heart had been strained. It was a mental change that caught Sheila's attention. The eyes had grown abnormally alert and cunning; there was nothing boyish or naïve left to the mouth; it was sinister, vengeful, unrelenting. He was in a wheel-chair between two husky giants of Australians who kept wary eyes upon him. As the surgeon and the nurse reached them, Monsieur Satan tossed his head back with a sudden recognition, and Sheila held out a friendly hand.

"I am glad to see you again, Captain Fauchet; not much of a scratch, I hope."

The eyes held their cunning, the sinister droop to the lips intensified as they curved mockingly to greet her: "Bon! It is Ma'am'selle O'Leary. The scratch it is nothing. Bertrand Fauchet has still the two good hands to kill with." He curled them as if over the hilts of invisible weapons, and with lightning thrusts attacked the air about him. "Une, deux, trois, quatre, cinq—Ha-ha!" and the appalling pantomime ended with a diabolical laugh.

In some inexplicable fashion he had come into full possession of his *nom de guerre*. Sheila had thought her nerves steel, her control unshakable; but she was shuddering when they reached the corridor. There she broke through the orthodox repression of her calling and quizzed the chief.

"What's happened? He wasn't like that when I knew him. If it was witch-times we'd say he'd been caught by the evil eye."

"Same thing, brought up to date. It's shell shock. Memory all right, nerves and brain speeded up like a maniac; he's come back obsessed with the idea he must kill. First night he was brought in, before we knew what the matter was, he knifed the two Germans in his ward. Since then we've kept him safe between these two Australians, but he has their nerves almost shattered." The chief smiled grimly.

To Sheila it seemed diabolically logical. What was more natural in this business of war than that when one's reason went over the top it should grip the mad desire to kill? But the horror of it! She turned back to the day's work white and sick at heart. For twenty-four hours she accepted it as inevitable. At the end of that time her memory was harkening back to the bashful boy of the French liner, the boy who could smile like a lost cherub, who looked at her with the fineness of soul that made her companionship a willing gift. Had that fine, simple part of him been blown to eternity and could eternity alone bring it back? And what of the years before him, the years such a physique was bound to claim? Did it mean a mad-cell with a keeper?

At the end of a third day the old Leerie of the San was walking through the wards of the hospital with her lamp trimmed and burning, casting such a radiance on that eager face that the men turned in their cots to catch the last look of her as she passed; and after she had gone blinked across at one another as if to say: "Did you see it? Did you feel it? And what was it, anyway?"

She was looking for some one; and she found him with a leg shot off, playing a mouth-organ in the farthest corner of one ward. He was a Chasseur Alpin; he had been wounded in the same charge as Monsieur Satan. Sheila was searching for cause and effect and she prayed this man might help her find them. As she sat down on the edge of the cot she thanked her particular star for a speaking knowledge of French. "Bon jour, mon ami. I have come for your help. C'est pour Capitaine Fauchet."

The mouth-organ dropped to the floor. The eyes that had been merely pleasantly retrospective gathered gloom. "Mais, que voulez-vous? All the others say it is hopeless. Tell me, ma'am'selle, what can I do?"

"I don't know—I hardly know what any of us can do. But we must try something. We know so little about shell shock, so often the impossible happens. Tell me, were you with him?"

The soldier hitched himself forward and leaned over on one elbow. "Toujours, ma'am'selle, always I am with him. Listen. I can tell you. I was born in the little town of Tourteron where Bertrand Fauchet was born—and where Nanette came to live with her brother Paul and their uncle, the good abbé. I was not of their class; but we all played together as children and even then Bertrand loved Nanette. The year war came they were betrothed. I am not tiring ma'am'selle?"

"No. Go on."

"We both enlisted in the Chasseurs Alpins. They made Bertrand a lieutenant, then a captain—he was a man to lead. And how kind, how good to his men! That was before he had won his nom de guerre—before they called him Monsieur Satan. If there was a danger he would see it first and race for it, to get ahead of his men. He would give them no orders that he would not fill with them; and always so pitying for the prisoners. 'Treat them kindly, mes garçons,' he would cry; and what mercy he would show! Mon Dieu! I have seen him, when his mouth was cracking with the thirst, pour the last drop from his canteen down the throat of a dying Boche, or share the last bread in his baluchon with a wounded prisoner. And the many times he has crept into No Man's Land to bring in a blessé we could hear moaning in the dark; and when it turned out a Boche, as so often it did, he would carry him with the same tenderness. That was Bertrand Fauchet when war began. Once I ask him, 'Why are you so careful with the Boches?' and he smiled that little-boy smile of his and say: 'Why not? We are still gentlemen if we are at war. And listen, François—some day our little Tourteron may fall into Boche hands. I would have them know many kindnesses from us before that happens.'

"Eh bien, Tourteron did fall into their hands, ma'am'selle, and there it has been until a fortnight ago. The German ranks swept it like a sea and made it their own, as they made the houses, the cattle, the orchards, the maids, quite their own. You comprehend? After that Bertrand fight like the devil and pray like the saint. Then one day a Boche stabs Paul—Nanette's brother Paul—as he stoops to succor him. Fauchet sees; and he hears the tales that come across the trenches to us. The abbé is crucified to the chapel door because he gives sanctuary to the young girls; Père Fauchet is shot in the Square with other anciens for example. After that Capitaine Fauchet gives us the order 'no mercy,' and we kill in battle and out. Ma'am'selle shudders—mais, que voulez-vous? He is Monsieur Satan now; but I still think he prays.

"And now comes the big drive of the Supreme Command. Village after village that has been Boche land for four years becomes French again. The people go mad with joy; they come rushing out to meet our regiments like souls turned out of hell by God Himself. But such souls, ma'am'selle! Be thankful in your heart you shall never have the little places of America thrown back to you by a retreating Boche army, never look into the faces of the people who have been made to serve their desires. It is like when the tide goes out on the coast and leaves behind it wreckage and slime. Only here it was human wreckage.

"At last the night came when we lay outside Tourteron. Bertrand called for me and we bivouacked together. We were to attack some time before dawn, after the moon had set. We could not trust our tongues—at such times things are better left unsaid; so we lay and smoked and prayed against what we feared. Only once Bertrand spoke—'François, to-morrow will see me always a devil or a saint, le bon Dieu knows which.'

"The moon shone bright till after midnight. We lay under cover of thin weeds, and beyond lay the meadow and stream and then the town. About twelve we heard the crisp bark of a sniper—two, three shots; then everything was still as death again. We were watching the shadows play across the meadow and timing the minutes before the moon would sink, when out of one of those shadows she came—straight across the meadow and the moonlight. It was Nanette, ma'am'selle. We knew it on the instant. She had a way of carrying the head and a step one could not forget. It was she the sniper had been after. One side of her face was crimson, the other side white and beautiful. But she did not seem to know, and the first look I had told me she had gone quite mad.

"I could feel Bertrand Fauchet stiffen by my side; I could feel him reach out for my Rosalie and grip it fast. Then he began a low or crooning call. He dared not call out loud—he dared not move to give our troops away! It was to be a surprise attack. So all he could do was to wait and call softly as to a little child, 'Nanette chérie, allons, allons!'

"There had been a skirmish in the meadow two days before; we had given way and the handful of dead we had left behind were still unburied. I think Nanette had heard that the Chasseurs Alpins had come and she had stolen out to find her lover. She came slowly, so slowly, and frail as a shadow herself. As she passed each corpse she knelt beside it and sang the foolish little berceuse that Poitou mothers sing to their babies. We could hear the humming far away, and as she came nearer we could hear the words. Ma'am'selle knows them, perhaps?

> "'Ah! Ah! papillon, marie-toi—
> Hélas, mon maître, je n'ai pas de quoi,
> La dans ma bergeri-e
> J'ai cent moutons; ça s'ra pour faire les noces de papillon.'"

"The first look I had told me she had gone quite mad"

The soldier crooned the song through to himself as if under the spell of the story he was telling. Then he went on. "She sang it through each time, patting the blue coats, pushing back the caps of those who still wore them, looking hard into each dead face. But she would always turn away with the little shake of the head, so triste, ma'am'selle. And all the time the man beside me calling out his heart in a whisper—'Nanette—Nanette—allons, chérie!'

"She was not twenty yards away, the arms of Bertrand Fauchet were reaching out to take her, when, pouf! the sniper barked again and Nanette went down like a pale cornflower before the reaper. And all the time we laid there, waiting for the moon to set. When we charge we charge like devils. We swept Tourteron clean of the Boches; *and we take no prisoners!* For that night every man remember the one thing, they love their captain and they see what he has seen. But before the day is gone we are sane men again, all but our captain. The shell that takes my leg takes what pity, what softness he has left, and leaves him with just the frenzy to kill. And it is not for me to wonder—moi—for I know all."

The story haunted Sheila for days; always when she closed her eyes she could see the girl Nanette coming across the meadow in the moonlight. She never failed to open them before she saw too far. The plaintive melody of the berceuse rang in her ears on duty and off, till at last she could stand it no longer. It was the old dominant Leerie who hunted up the chief.

"Colonel Sparks, I want you to put me on Captain Fauchet's case. The work is lighter now; you can do with one less operating-room. I know it's bad form to interfere, but I want my chance on that case."

The chief looked his surprise. "I've heard of your fondness for breaking rules—wondered when you were going to begin. I don't mind giving you up, but that case is hopeless. I'm sure of it. Listen—and this isn't for publication—Fauchet got out of his ward again, hid in the corridors until the nurse was gone, and killed another German last night. That man is incurably insane and we can't keep him here any longer."

"Please!" There was a look about Leerie that could not be denied, a compelling prayer for the right to save another human being. "You could keep him a little longer; I'll promise there'll be no more dead Germans. Give me my chance."

"What's your idea?"

The girl raised a deprecating hand. "Something so crazy that you'd laugh at it. Let me keep it to myself—and give me Captain Fauchet."

In the end Leerie had her wish. The little room at the end of a ward, used heretofore for supplies, was turned into a private room, and Monsieur Satan was moved in, with Sheila O'Leary as guardian. It was very evident that the patient approved. Once the door was closed behind them, he beckoned the nurse to him with malignant joy.

"They are all Germans out there—I've just discovered it. Sooner or later they will all have to be destroyed. You are an American. I can swear to that, for I saw you on a liner coming from America and your French is so bad, pardonnez-moi, it could not be anything but American. That is why I trust you. You are with me against the Boches, n'est-ce pas?"

Sheila solemnly agreed.

"Eh bien, listen. The world is slowly turning Boche. You pour a little Pinard into water and what do you get? Crimson! Well, you scatter a few

Boches over the earth and what have you? A German world colored Prussian blue. Come closer, ma'am'selle." He put out nervous hands and drew her down so he could whisper his words. "And the cure, ma'am'selle, the cure? Ah, moi, Monsieur Satan, knows it."

They spent the rest of the day in discussing the killing qualities of shells, grenades, bombs; the stabbing qualities of bayonets, daggers, swords; the exploding properties of dynamite, nitroglycerin, TNT, and others. As they talked Monsieur Satan sucked in his breath exultantly and hissed between his teeth, "*Zigouille, toujours zigouille!*" while his hand stabbed and twisted into the air.

Another day and he had taken Sheila entirely into his confidence. "I have my mind made. You shall hear the cure, ma'am'selle, for you and I will be partners. A Boche world can be cured but the one way—destroyed, completely destroyed," and he laughed uproariously. Then his eyes narrowed; he was all cunning and intensity, a beast of prey crouched for the spring. "Ah, but we must whisper; there are spies everywhere. The men in the wards are all spies pretending they are French wounded; and the doctors are spies. Oh, the Boches are damnably clever, but we will be more damnable—we will outwit them. We will blow them into a million atoms. They will make good fertilizer for French vineyards in a hundred years. Eh bien?"

So Sheila became partner in evolving the most colossal crime the world had ever known. Everything played into her hands and gave credence to her deceptions. The great cases that came by night packed with dressings were to Monsieur Satan air-bombs with propellers. They were to be set loose on the day appointed in such millions that the air would be charged with them, the sun blotted out; and they would drop in exploding masses over the earth, exterminating humanity.

"They shall be like the hordes of locusts that nearly destroyed Egypt—only these shall destroy. And how every one shall run in terror! You will see, ma'am'selle. It will be a good sight." And Monsieur Satan rubbed his hands in keen anticipation.

The tanks of oxygen placed on motor-trucks, the gasoline-tanks, were nothing else than a deadly gas. The partners had concocted it out of the strangest compounds, unshed-tears, heart-agony, fear-in-the-night, snipers' barks, and moonshine. Monsieur Satan chuckled over the formula and said he would swear not a living soul could withstand a single whiff of it. It was agreed that the makers of the gas—mythological beings Sheila had created—should be killed at once so that their secret should never be discovered; and Sheila herself was despatched to compass the deed. Before she returned the bell in the church near by was tolling for their parting souls; and Monsieur Satan chuckled as he cast admiring glances at this prompt executioner.

"You are a good pupil, ma'am'selle; you learn quickly. Now the maps." And they fell to diagraming where the piping for this deadly gas should be laid.

Not an inch of the old world was to be left peopled; from east to west and north to south everything was to be destroyed. No, not everything. Even as Monsieur Satan decreed it he hesitated. "There are the children, I think—yes, I think they shall live. Their hearts are pure; the Boches cannot contaminate them. They shall live after us with no memory of evil, so they can build again the beautiful world." He stopped and looked across at the nurse with a haunting, wistful stare. "Tell me, ma'am'selle, was the world ever beautiful?"

"Very beautiful, capitaine."

He passed an uncertain hand over his eyes. "I seem to remember that it was; but now I see it always running with red blood boiling from hell."

After that the children were always in his mind; as he planned the destruction of the rest of the world he planned their re-creation. Thereupon Sheila saw to it that the war orphans from the *crêche* came to play in the hospital gardens—under the window of the little room. Soon it became a custom for Monsieur Satan to look for them, to ask their names, and wave gaily to them. And they waved back. And the chief of the surgical staff began to marvel that Monsieur Satan should give no more trouble.

Among them was a little girl, a wan, ethereal little creature who sat apart from the other children and watched their play with far-away, haunting eyes, as if she wondered what in the world they were doing. Sheila had found toys for her—a ball, a doll, a jumping-jack—and tried to coax her to play. But she only clung to them for their rare value as possessions; as a means to enjoyment they were quite meaningless. From one of the older children Sheila got her story. Her father had been killed, her mother was with the Boches; there was no one else. With an aching heart the nurse wondered how many thousand Madelines France held.

One day she brought the child in to Monsieur Satan and repeated her story. He listened wisely, patting her on the head, and then whispered to Sheila: "Ah, what did I say! These Boches—they get everything—the mothers, the sweethearts." Then to Madeline: "Listen, ma pauvre; you shall have the sadness no longer. Monsieur Satan will promise you happiness, ah, such happiness in the new beautiful world he is preparing for you. Now go. But 'sh ... sh! You must say nothing."

From this moment Sheila became senior partner. It was she who suggested all the extraordinary horrors Monsieur Satan had overlooked. It was she who speeded up time and plans. "I have the hospitals and streets all mined in case the flying bombs should not come thick enough; and I have the wells poisoned. Isn't that a clever idea?"

The man looked disturbed. "That's as clever as the Boches. But the children—where will they drink? You must take care of the children."

Then Sheila played her trump card and said the thing she had been waiting so long to say. Like Monsieur Satan she hissed the words between her teeth, while her face took on all the diabolical cunning it could muster. "The children—bah! What do they matter, after all? I have decided—the children shall be destroyed."

Monsieur Satan sprang from his chair. He pinioned her arms behind her, forcing her back so he could look deep into her eyes with all the hate and mercilessness his soul harbored. "Touch Madeline—the children, never! Let so much as one little hair of their heads be harmed and I—Monsieur Satan—will kill you!"

She left him with a non-committal shrug, left him panting and swearing softly under his breath.

From that moment he watched Sheila suspiciously and followed the children with jealous eyes. For Madeline he called constantly; and she sat on his knee by the hour while he danced the jumping-jack outrageously and taught her to sing to the doll a certain foolish berceuse that Poitou mothers sing to their babies.

Sheila had planned to stage their day of destruction with the craft of a master manager. She had had to take certain officials into her confidence and get the chief to sign such orders as had never been issued in a hospital before. But in the end Fate staged it, and did it infinitely better than the nurse had even conceived it. The hour of doom struck a full half-day too soon—the children were playing in the gardens, under Monsieur Satan's window instead of being in the cellar of the *crèche* as he had decreed; and Sheila was helping another head nurse do dressings in the ward outside.

There were only a few minutes after the siren blew before the first of the great Fokkers appeared over the city. Monsieur Satan's mind went strangely blank; the children stopped their play and gaped stupidly into the sky; Sheila did nothing but listen. Then the bombs began to rain down on the city. The noise was terrific. The children ran aimlessly about, shrieking pitifully. It was this that set Monsieur Satan's mind to working again. He broke out of the little room like the madman he was. He might have been Lucifer himself as he stumbled along on his bandaged foot, his hair erect, his eyes blazing a thousand inextinguishable fires. In the corridor he came upon Sheila, with other nurses and doctors, hurrying to gather in the out-of-door patients. As he overtook them a bomb struck the hospital.

"Sacrebleu!" he shouted. "You bungler! you fool of a destroyer! It was not the hour—and the children—First I go to save them. Afterward I come to kill you, ma'am'selle."

He was out before them all, through the entrance and down the steps, when another bomb struck. The doorway and the pillars were crushed to gravel and Monsieur Satan was hurled headlong across the gardens. In an instant he was up, stumbling frantically toward the children, his arms outstretched in appealing vindication to those small, quivering faces turned to him in their hour of annihilation. "Mes enfants, have no fear. I come—I come."

A third bomb fell. The children were tumbled in a heap like a pile of jackstraws. Monsieur Satan had time enough to see them go down before a fourth followed with the quick precision of an automatic. Yes, he saw; and in that horror-smiting moment believed it all a part of his great scheme of destruction; then the universe went to pieces about him and something crumbled inside his brain. He stood transfixed to the earth, staring helplessly in front of him, as immovable as a graven image.

It is one of the anomalies of war that the things that apparently destroy sometimes re-create. The gigantic impact of exploding masses may destroy a man's hearing, his sight, his memory, or his mercy, and leave him thus maimed for all time. But it happens, sometimes, that the first shock is followed by another which restores with the suddenness of a miracle and makes the man whole again. That delicate bit of human mechanism which has been battered out of place is battered in, by the merest chance.

So it was with Monsieur Satan; and when Sheila and the chief found him he was rubbing his eyes as children will who wake and find themselves in strange places. He saw only the chief at first and tried to pull himself together.

"Ah, monsieur, I think some things have happened—but I cannot as yet make the full report. I am Bertrand Fauchet, Chasseur Alpin," and he tried to click his bandaged heel against his shoe. Then he looked beyond and saw Sheila. It was as if he was seeing her for the first time since they had separated at the French quay. "Bon Dieu! It is Ma'am'selle O'Leary." He held out a shaking hand. "We meet in the thick of war—is it not so?"

His eyes left Sheila and traveled apprehensively to the children. They were wriggling themselves free of one another; frightened and bruised, but not hurt, barring one. The smallest of them all lay on the outskirts of the heap, quite motionless.

"If you will permit," Monsieur Satan stumbled on and gently picked up Madeline. He looked all compassion and bewilderment. "I do not altogether understand, ma'am'selle. But this little girl, I should like to carry her to some hospital and see that all is well with her. I seem to remember that she belongs to me." He smiled apologetically at the two watching him, then stumbled ahead with his burden.

At the base hospital they gave Sheila O'Leary full credit for the curing of Bertrand Fauchet, which, of course, she flatly denied. She laid it entirely to the interference of Fate and a child. But the important thing is that Bertrand Fauchet left the hospital a sound man—and that Madeline went with him, each holding fast to the hand of the other.

"She is mine now," he said, as he took leave of Sheila. "Le bon Dieu saw fit to send me in the place of that other papa. Eh, p'tite?" He stroked the hair back from the little face that looked worshipfully up at him. "It is for us who remember to make these little ones forget. N'est-ce pas, ma'am'selle? And we are going back to the world together, to find somewhere the happiness and the great love for Madeline. Adieu."

Chapter VII

THE LAD WHO OUTSANG THE STARS

IN the American Military Hospital No. 10 one could always count on Ward 7-A beginning the day with a genuine fanfare of good spirits—that is to say, ever since that ward had acquired a distinction and personality of its own. On this particular morning the doors of the wards were open, for orderlies were scrubbing floors, and Sheila O'Leary in the operating-room above could catch the words of the third chorus that had rung through the hospital since the ban of silence had been raised.

> "Gra-ma-cree ma-cruiskeen, Slainte-geal ma-vour-neen,
> Gra-ma-cree a-coolin bawn, bawn, bawn,
> Oh!"

As usual, Larry's crescendo boomed in the lead. How those lads could sing!

In the regular order of things it was time for dressings; but the regular order of things was so often broken at No. 10 that it had nearly become a myth. The operating staff had been steadily at it since eleven the night before. If nothing more came in, they might be through by eleven now and the dressings come only two hours late. That would be rare good luck. Under the spell of the singing the tired backs of surgeons and nurses straightened unconsciously; cramped muscles seemed to lose some of their kinks; everybody smiled without knowing it—down to the last of the boys who were waiting their turn in the corridor outside. The boys had not been in the hospital long enough to know anything about Ward 7-A, but the challenge to courage and good spirits in that chorus of voices was too dominant to be denied, even among the sorest wounded of them. One after another rallied to it like veterans.

"Gra-ma-cree ma-cruiskeen bawn," boomed Larry's voice to the finish.

The chief of the Surgical Staff looked at Sheila as she handed him the sutures he was reaching for. "They're the best we've had yet, eh? Not one with half a fighting chance, and just listen to the ones who are pulling through."

"They're Irish." There was a tinge of pride in the nurse's voice.

The chief smiled. "It's like flipping a coin to find out whether you're more Irish or American. Sometimes it's heads, sometimes it's tails. Which is it, honestly?"

"Honestly, both!" Sheila laughed softly. Then the door opened to admit the last of the stretchers, and she sobered for an instant until she saw the faces of the boys. She knew why they were smiling, and her eyes shone in the old luminous, Leerie fashion as she greeted them, each as if he had been an old friend.

"There's a welcome for you. Those lads you hear have gone through what you are going through, only a lot worse. Listen, and think of that as you go under. They'll be singing again in a moment." And as she slipped the ether cone over the face of the first, up from Ward 7-A in rollicking cadences came another chorus:

> "Wi' me bundle on me shoulder, sure, there's not a
> man that's bolder—
> I am leavin' dear old Ireland without warnin'.
> For I've lately took the notion for to cross the briny
> ocean,
> An' I'm off for Philadelphia in the mornin'."

The smile on the face of the first boy spread to a grin under its covering of gauze. "I'm off for Philadelphia, too," he mumbled, thickly, and the eyes that looked into Sheila's for a few last nebulous seconds showed all the comfortable security of a child's.

They were hard at it for another hour, and while Sheila O'Leary's hands flew from sterilizer to ether cone, from handing instruments and holding forceps to tying sutures and packing wounds, her mind was busy with something that lay far beyond. To this girl, who had come across to do her bit, life had become a jumble of paradoxes. She had come to give, out of the bounty of her skill and her womanhood; instead she had received far more abundantly from the largess of universal brotherhood and sacrifice. She had come to minister, and she had been ministered unto by every piece of human wreckage swept across the door-sill of the hospital. She had thought to dispense life, and to her ever-increasing wonder she had been given a life so boundless that it reached beyond all previous dreams of space or time. She was learning what thousands had been learning since the war began, those who had thrown their fortunes into its crucible, and that is that if anything comes out at all, it comes out in the form of spirit and not of flesh.

Back in the old days at the sanitarium she had felt herself bound only to the problems and emergencies of war. It had never occurred to her then that in an incredibly short time she would be bothering about matters of adjustment afterward. With peace already on the horizon, she was troubled a hundredfold more than she had been when indefinite war was the promise for the future. From the beginning she had marveled at the buoyancy and optimism of the men who were focusing their lives within the limits of each day. Many of them never thought in terms of more than twenty-four hours; often it was less. They had learned the knack of intensive living. World-old truths were flashed into their minds like spotlights; friends were made and lost in a few hours; eternity was visioned and compassed in a minute. The last words Jerry Donoghue of Ward 7-A had said before he went west came back to Sheila with a curious persistence.

"When all's said and done, miss, it's been a grand life—Brave lads for comrades—a lass who kept faith to the end—a good fight an' somethin' good to fight for—Near five years of it—wi' perdition grinnin' ye in the face an' the Holy Mother walkin' at your back—Sure, I might ha' lived fifty year in Letterkenny an' never tasted life half so plentiful—or—so—sweet."

That was the strange part of it; they had all found life "plentiful an' sweet"—nurses, surgeons, soldiers alike. They might be homesick, worn out with the business of fighting and patching up afterward, eternally aching in body and heart with the long stretches of horror and work with little sleep and less food, and yet not a handful out of every thousand of them would have chosen to quit if they could.

But when the quitting-time came, when war was over, what was going to happen then? Sheila wondered it about the boys who lay unconscious on their stretchers, packed in the room about her. She wondered it about the boys conscious in their cots below. Most of all she wondered it about Ward 7-A. It was going to hurt so many to have to look beyond the immediate day into a procession of numberless days stretching into years and years. The sudden relaxing from big efforts to little ones, that would hurt, too, like the uncramping of over-strained muscles. And the being thrown back on oneself to think, to act, to feel for oneself again—what of that? It was like dismembering a gigantic machine and scattering the infinitesimal parts of it broadcast over the earth to function alone. Only many of the parts would be imperfect, and all would have souls to reckon with.

But of the puzzle of it one fact stood out grippingly vital to Sheila. No soul must be thrown out of the melting-pot back into the old accustomed order of life and be left to feel unfit or unnecessary. There must be a big, compelling place for every man who came home. Of all the tragedies of war, she could conceive no greater one than to have these men who had put no limit to the price they were willing to pay to make the world safe for democracy sent back useless, to mark time to eternity.

But who was going to keep this from happening? How were the thousands of mutilés to be made free of the burden of dependence and toleration? Who was going to guard them against atrophy of spirit? The nurse gathered up the last of the instruments and threw them in the sterilizer. As she took off her apron and wiped the beads of sweat from her face, her chief eyed her suspiciously.

"Get your coffee before you touch those dressings in 7-A. Understand? When did you have your clothes off last?" He growled like a good-natured but spent old dog.

The girl gave her uniform a disgusted look. "Pretty bad, isn't it? I put it on four—no, five days ago, but I've had my shoes off twice." She laid an impulsive hand on the chief's arm. "Promise about the coffee if you'll promise to do the dressings with me instead of Captain Griggs. He calls them the 'down-and-outers.' I can't quite stand for that."

"Well, what would you call 'em?"

"The invincibles," she declared. "Wouldn't you?"

But for all her promise, Sheila O'Leary did not get past the door of 7-A without putting in her head and calling out a "good morning." Whereupon twelve Irish tongues, dripping almost as many brogues, flung it back at her with a vengeance.

There were thirteen of them, all told, the remnants of a company of Royal Irish that had crossed the Scheldt with Haig. As Larry Shea had put it on the day of their arrival, they "made as grand leavin's as one could expect under the circumstances." The ambulances that had brought them, along with the additional seven who had gone west, had pivoted wrong at one of the crossroads, so that the American Military Hospital No. 10 had fallen heir to them instead of the B. H. T. It is recorded that even the chief showed consternation when he looked them over, and Larry, catching the look and being the only man conscious at the time, snorted indignantly:

"Well, sir, if ye think we're a mess, ye should have seen the Fritzies we left behind. Furninst them we're an ordther of perfectly decent lads." And Larry had crumpled up into a grinning unconsciousness.

It was Larry who led the singing; it was Larry now who, with an eye on the one silent figure in the ward and another on the nurse in the doorway, threw a wheedling remark to hold her with them a moment "by way of heartenment to Jamie." "Wait a bit, miss. Patsy MacLean was just askin' were ye a good hand at layin' a ghost?"

Before Sheila could answer, Harrigan, an Irish-American orderly, stepped over the threshold and shook a fist at 7-A.

"Aw, cut it out. The way this bunch works Miss O'Leary makes me sick. Don't cher know she hasn't been off duty for twenty-four hours? Let her go, can't cher?"

Johnnie O'Neil, from the far end of the room, smiled the smile of a cherub. "An' don't ye know, laddie, that it's always the saints in heaven that has the worst sinners on their hands? 'Tis jealous ye are, not being wicked enough to get a bit more of her attention yerself."

Sheila smiled impartially at them both, and with a parting promise of dressings to come she hurried off. Ward 7-A settled itself to wait for the worst and the best that the day had to offer. The room was a very small one, and the thirteen cots barely crowded into it, with space at the foot for Jamie O'Hara's wheel-chair to go the length and turn. They had been kept together by Sheila's urgent plea that they should be given a ward to themselves instead of scattering them through the larger wards, and it is doubtful if in all the war a more quietly merciful act had been executed. Not one of the thirteen but would have scorned to show any sign of dependence on the others, yet intuitively the girl had guessed what they would be able to give one another in the matter of spiritual succor. The way they continually hectored and teased, matched wits and good humor, as they had matched strength and daring in the old fighting-days before the hospital, was meat and drink to the souls struggling for dominance over mutilated bodies. United, they were men; separated—Sheila had often shuddered to think what pitiful, pain-tortured beings they might have been.

When she returned to the ward the chief was with her, and their combined arrival brought forth a prolonged, fortissimoed wail shammed forth in good Gaelic fashion. Larry's great hairy arm shot out, and a vindictive forefinger was wagged in the direction of the third cot.

"Ye'd best begin with Patsy MacLean this day. He hasn't been laid out first in a fortnight."

The others, taking the words from Larry's tongue, chorused, "Aye, begin wi' Patsy, the devil take him!"

"Why the devil? Wouldn't Fritzie do as well?" The chief smiled indulgently upon them all.

"'Tis a case for the devil, this time. Tell the colonel what you were putting over us last night," Michael Kenney, lance-corporal, growled through an undercurrent of chuckle.

Patrick MacLean, the color-sergeant, grinned as he reached out a welcoming hand to both surgeon and nurse. He was a prime favorite with them, as with his own lads. When pain wrestled for the upper hand, when things went wrong, moods turned black, or nights stretched interminably long and unendurable, Patsy could always turn the trick and produce something so absorbingly interesting or ridiculous that the pain and the long nights were forgotten. How well Sheila remembered that first time they had dressed his wounds! The muscles had stood out on his arms like whipcords; sweat poured down his face. He fainted twice, each time coming round to drawl out his story in that unforgetable Irish way:

"We were dthrivin' them afore us like sheep, all so tame an' sociable I was forgettin' where I was. Somehow the notion took me I was back on the moorlan' drivin' the flocks for my father, when a Fritzie overhead drops a bomb on our captain.... It spatters the mud in my eyes somethin' terrible, an' when I rubs them clean again the machine-guns were cacklin' all round us like a parcel o' hens layin' eggs; we'd stumbled on a nest of them. Holy Pether, I was mad! I was for stickin' the colors in the muzzle o' one o' their bloody guns, an' I sings out as I rush 'em, 'Erin go bragh!' Then down I goes. Culmullen, there, comes staggerin' up. 'Take the colors,' says I. 'I've got no legs to carry 'em on.' 'I can't,' says he; 'I've got no arms to shoulder 'em.'... A bit aftherwards I sees Jamie—he's second in command—come runnin' up wild, but his arms an' legs is still in pairs, so I shouts afore things go black, 'The colors, Jamie, ye take the colors.' 'Wish to God, Patsy, I could,' says he, 'but I can't see.'... Faith, weren't we a healthy lot, miss? An' we the Royal Irish!" He had grinned then as he was grinning now.

Culmullen in the next cot, a schoolmaster from Ballygowan, raised his head. "Miss O'Leary, Patsy's the worst liar in Ulster. Ye might keep that in mind whenever he has anything to tell. If I had had the schooling of ye, I'd have thrashed the thruth into ye, ye rascal! Will ye kindly lean over and brush the hair out of my eyes, and if ye tickle my nose this time, I'll have Larry thrash ye for me the instant he's up."

The color-sergeant pulled himself over and gently brushed back the straggling hair. "Such a purty lad!" he murmured, sarcastically. "What's an arm or two so long's the Fritzies didn't ruin one o' them handsome features—nor shorten the length o' your tongue."

"What is it this time, Sergeant?" Sheila spoke coaxingly as she bent to the dressings.

"Well, ye know I've said from the beginnin' 'twas no ways natural havin' them legs o' mine twistin' an' achin' same as if they were still hangin' onto me. I leave it to both of yez. If they'd been anyways decent legs an' considerate o' the kindness I've always shown them, wouldn't they have quit pestherin' me when they took Dutch leave?"

"Stop moralizin'," shouted Johnnie O'Neil, the piper from Antrim. "Get down to the p'int o' your tale."

"It hasn't any point: it's flat," growled the lance-corporal.

Unembarrassed, Patsy MacLean went on: "I was a-thinkin' this all over again last night, a-listenin' to the ambulances comin' in, when a breath o' wind pushes the door open a bit, an' in walks, as natural as life, the ghost o' them two legs. 'Tis the gospel truth I'm tellin' ye. They walked a bit bowlegged, same as they always did, straight through the door an' down the ward. An' the queer thing is they never stopped by Larry's cot or Casey Ryan's—the heathen!—but came right on to me."

"Faith, they wouldn't have had the nerve to stop. The leg Casey lost was as straight as a hazel wand, same as mine." Larry snorted contemptuously.

"The two of yez are jealous." Patsy lowered his voice to a mock whisper and confided to the chief and Sheila, "They know they'll have to be buyin' a good pair o' shoes an' throwin' the odd away, while I'll be sayin' enough from the shoes I'll never have to be buyin' to keep mysel' in cigars for the rest o' my life."

"But Patsy's wondtherin' can ye lay the ghost, miss?" Timothy Brennan, who had lost the "cream of his face," repeated the question Larry had asked a half-hour before. The rest of the ward tittered expectantly.

"Let me see—" The Irish blood in her steadied the nurse's hands, while she drew her lips into quizzical solemnity and winked at Culmullen over her shoulder. "I always thought it was restlessness that sent ghosts walking. Maybe these have come back, looking for their boots."

The titter broke into a roar of delight. "Thrue for ye!" shouted Parley-voo Flynn, pounding the arm of Jamie's chair with his one fist. "All ye've got to do, Patsy, is to be puttin' your boots beside your chair onct more, an' them legs will scrooch comfortably into them an' never haunt ye again. The lass is right, isn't she, Jamie?"

Eleven pairs of eyes and an odd one shifted apprehensively from the lad who was being dressed to the lad in the wheel-chair, and the eyes all showed varying degrees of trouble, uncertainty, and sorrow. They had a way of searching Jamie out in this fashion many times a day, while he sat very still, with eyes bandaged and lips that never flinched but never broke to a smile.

Larry shook a hairy fist at Parley-voo and answered the question himself:

"Of course she's right! Isn't she always? An' who but a heathen would be doubtin' the manners of a ghost?"

"Aye, but where will I be gettin' the boots?" Patsy made a sour grimace. "Me own purty ones had Christian burial somewhere back in that tremendous mud-puddle. Would any gentleman, now, still havin' two good legs, give me the loan of his boots for one night? Size eleven, if I don't disremember."

"That's Teig's number. Lend him yours, Teig, like a good lad, or we'll never be rid o' them ghosts." Mat O'Shaughnessy, at the other end of the line, fairly shook with the depth of his wail.

Teig Magee chuckled. He had lost an inch or so of back and was waiting the glad day when they could mend it with an inch or so of shin-bone; in the mean time he was paralyzed. "Say, Docthor, would ye mind reachin' undther my pillow an' fetchin' them out for me? The lads have a way of forgettin' my hands are temporarily engaged. Thank ye. Ye can have them, Patsy, but ye'll have to go bail your ghosts won't up an' thramp off wi' them entirely."

It ended by the schoolmaster giving security—a half-crown with a bullet hole through it. Sheila was appointed custodian, and the boots were placed beside the color-sergeant's cot "against the comin' night."

As the chief and Sheila passed on from cot to cot, the spirits of Ward 7-A never wavered. Johnnie, who had piped the lads into battle and out for four years, and who daily rejoiced over the fact that Fritzie had shown the good sense to take a foot instead of a hand, told them that he was in rare luck now, for there would be time to make wee Johnnie at home the grandest piper in all of Ireland—an honor he could never have promised himself before.

There was "Bertha" Milliken, named for the big gun he had put out of commission and the gun crew he had captured. He had been given the V. C. for that. His pet joke was telling how the Fritzies grudged him its possession by shooting it away on the Scheldt along with a good bit that was under it. The nurse and surgeon handled "Bertha" very carefully; there was no knowing just what was going to happen to him. Casey Ryan had lost the odd of 'most everything the Lord had started him with, as he put it. An eye, an ear, a lung, and a leg were gone, and he was beating all the others at getting well. Mat O'Shaughnessy had it in the "vital." He was continuously boasting that it was the handiest place of all, and if it didn't get him he'd be the only perfect specimen invalided home.

"Parley-voo," the only one of them who essayed French, had wounds many but inconspicuous. He was given to counting a hypothetical fortune that might be his if the Empire would give him a shilling for every time he had been hit. Joseph Daly and "Gospel" Smith, the one Methodist, carried head wounds, while "Granny" Sullivan, the oldest, wisest, and most comforting of the company, had one smashed hip and a hole through the other, "the devil of a combination." Never had the atmosphere of 7-A been keener or spicier. Jamie alone sat still and silent.

Jamie was the last to be dressed, and because there was little to do the chief slipped away and left him to Sheila. As the nurse passed from Mat's cot to the wheel-chair, eleven pairs of eyes and an odd one followed her. A hush fell suddenly on the ward. The lads never intended this should happen, but somehow, at the same time everyday, the silence gripped them, and they seemed powerless to stay it. It was "Granny" Sullivan who first threw it off.

"'Tis a grand day outside, Jamie. Maybe ye're feeling the sun, now, comin' through the window?"

The nurse had lifted the bandage from the eyes. There was nothing there but empty sockets, almost healed. One could hear the quick intake of breath from the watching twelve, while every face registered an agony it had scorned to show for its own disablement. But for Jamie, "the singing lad from Derry" as they lovingly called him, it was different. They could face their own conditions with amazing jocularity, but they writhed daily under the torment of Jamie's. They could brave it no better than could he. For to put eternal darkness on the lad who loved the light, who would sit spellbound before the play of colors in the east at dawn or the flash of moonlight across troubled water, who could make a song out of the smile of a child or the rhythm of flying birds in the sky, that was damnable. An arch-fiend might have conceived it, but where was God to let it happen? A crippled Jamie without an arm or a leg was endurable—that cried out for no blasphemy—but a Jamie without eyes—God in heaven, how could it be!

The face of the singing lad was the face of a dreamer, as exquisite as a piece of marble that might have been fashioned by Praxiteles for a sun god. Since the battle on the Scheldt it had become a white mask, shorn of all dreams. Almost it might have been a death-mask for the soul of Jamie O'Hara. It showed no response now when "Granny" spoke; only the lad's hands fluttered a moment toward the window, then dropped heavily back into his lap.

"Aye, maybe I feel it." The voice was colorless and tired. "I can't be remembering clear sunlight any more. The last days of the fighting, smoke was too thick in the sky, or the rains fell."

Eleven pairs of eyes and one odd one cast about for some inspiration. "Sure, think o' somethin' pleasanter nor cannon smoke an' rain. Think o'—" "Granny" floundered for a moment, then gave up in despair.

"That's all I see when I look up. When I look down, it's worse—an everlasting earth, covered with mud and dying men!" Jamie shivered.

Larry struggled out of his torment. "I say, Jamie, don't ye mind the song ye were makin' for us the day we fell back from Cambrai? 'Twas an Irish one, full o' the sun an' the singin' birds of Donegal. Wi' the Fritzies risin' like a murdtherous tide behind us, 'twas all that kept the heart in us that day. Ye say it for Miss O'Leary. Sure, ye've never said a song for her yet."

Jamie shook his head. "I'm sorry, lad; I've lost it. I was making so many songs those days—ye couldn't be expecting a body to carry them all about in his head. Now could ye?" The lips tried bravely to smile, and failed again.

But Larry grinned triumphantly. "Sure 'Granny' has it wrote down. He showed it to me once. Fetch it, 'Granny,' an' let Jamie be re—" He broke off, aghast; the lads about him were staring in absolute horror. Only the singing lad showed nothing. He might not have heard, or, hearing, the words were meaningless.

So Sheila took matters into her own hands. She covered the eyes with fresh gauze, wrapped Jamie up, and bundled him out in his chair to Harrigan with the remark that the day was too fine to miss and there was more of it outside the hospital than in. She watched until she had seen Harrigan take him to a sunny, wind-sheltered corner of the gardens, and then she came back to 7-A. She was thinking of Peter Brooks, her man at the front, and she was trying to fathom with all her heart what manner of healing she would give had Peter come back to her as Jamie O'Hara had come. She closed the door of the ward behind her and faced the twelve.

"Lads, what are we going to do for Jamie?"

Larry groaned out loud. It was the first luxury of expression he had indulged in since Jamie had been wheeled out. "Aye, what are we goin' to do? That's what every man of us has been askin' himself since—since he knew."

"We act like a crowd o' half-wits, a-thryin' to boost his spirits a bit, an' all the time he grows whiter an' quieter." Patsy turned his head away; his lips were twitching.

"Aye, that's God's truth." "Bertha's" hoarse croak was heavy with despair. "Ye can see for yourself, miss, it's noways nat'ral for Jamie—that's the worst of it. It's been Jamie, just, that always put heart back in us when things went blackest. Wasn't it him that made it easy goin' for them that went west? Can one of us mind the time he wasn't ready with a song to fetch us over the top, or through the mud—or straight to death, if them was the orders? No matter how loud the guns screeched, we could always hear Jamie above them."

"We could hear him when we couldn't have heard another sound," Culmullen mumbled.

"Gospel" Smith raised a bandaged head and leveled piercing eyes at Sheila. "You know what the Gospel says about the stars singing in the morning—all together like? Well, Jamie was the lad who could outsing them. You know how it feels at that gray, creepy hour o' dawn, when a man's heart jumps to his throat and sticks there, and his hands shake like a girl's? Often's the time we'd be waiting orders to attack just like that. The stars might have shouted themselves clear o' the sky, for all the good they'd have done us; but Jamie was different. He'd make us a couplet or a verse to sing low under our breath, something you could put your teeth into. And when the orders came our hearts were always back where the Lord had put them."

"Granny" Sullivan plucked nervously at his blanket. "An' now, when we want to hearten him, we're hurtin' instead. Seems as if the devil took hold of our tongues an' spilled the wrong words off."

"Shall I tell you what I would try to do, if I were one of you Irish lads who had fought with him?" Sheila's face was as drawn as any of the twelve.

"In God's name tell us!" Johnnie, the piper, spoke as reverently as if he were at mass.

"You heard what he said just now about seeing nothing but mud and dying men? Well, that's the trouble. He can't see any longer things he loves, the things he has always carried in his heart. All the beautiful memories have been lost, and all he has left are the horrors of those last days. He's got nothing left to make into songs any more. Don't you see? You've got to bring that back to him, that power to see—here." The girl's hand pressed her heart.

"Aye, but how?" Patsy asked it breathlessly.

"Bring him back his memories—memories of Ireland, of the things he loved best to sing about. You have eyes; make him see."

A hush fell on Ward 7-A. Then Timothy Brennan muttered as a man alone: "'Tis the words of a woman. God's blessin' on her!"

All through the day there rang through Sheila's ears the last words Jamie had said to her that morning. He had turned his face back, as Harrigan had wheeled him away, to answer her "All right, Jamie?" with "As right as ever I'll be. Do ye know, the O'Haras are famous for their long living? My grandfather lived to be ninety-eight, and his father to be over a hundred. That leaves me seventy-five years, maybe. Seventy-five years! And already I'm fearin' the length of a day." She was still hearing them when she came back to the ward at day's end to find Jamie in his old accustomed place by the window. His face was as masklike as ever, and Larry was talking:

"Sure, I mind often an' often how the neighbors used to tell me if I'd lie asleep with my ear to a fairy rath I'd be hearin' their music an' seein' their dancin'. But I never did. But I saw a sight as grand, the flight o' the skylark at ring-o'-day. Many's the time I've seen them leave the marsh an' go liltin' into the blue."

"And the lilting!" Culmullen closed his eyes the better to recall it. "I mind the last time I heard one. The sky was turned orange, and the lough turned gold. The marsh was glistening with mist, and out of the reeds where her nest was she flew. It was like a feathered bundle of song thrown skyward."

"Aye, what a song!" Johnnie, the piper, spoke with ecstasy. "Hark! I can make it." He puckered his lips, and through them came the sweet, lilting notes of the lark's matin song.

"Make it again." Jamie was leaning forward in his chair, his hands gripping the arms.

Again the piper whistled it through, and then again and again. A smile brushed Jamie's lips, and the others, watching, breathless, saw.

"What is it?" asked "Granny," softly.

"Naught. Only for the moment I was thinking I could be smelling the dew on the bogs, yonder. Can ye pipe for the blackbirds, Johnnie?"

And Johnnie piped.

So a new order of things was established in Ward 7-A, and as heretofore the lads had vied in witty derision of their calamities they vied now with one another in telling tales of Ireland. Each marshaled forth his dearest, greenest memory, clothed in its best, to fill the ears and heart of Jamie O'Hara. Sometimes he smiled, and then there was a great, silent rejoicing among the twelve; sometimes he asked for more, and then tongues tripped over one another in mad effort to furnish forth a memory more wonderful than all that had gone before. But more often he sat still and white, as if he heard nothing. And in the midst of it all, as the lads drew each day nearer to health, Sheila noted a new uneasiness among them. It was Larry who spoke the trouble while the nurse was doing his dressings. He whispered it, so the others should not hear.

"By rights we don't belong here. Well, they'll be movin' us soon as we're mended, won't they?"

The nurse nodded.

"Invalided home. Ye know what that means?"

Again the nurse nodded.

"Mind ye, there's been never a word dropped atween us, but we're all fearin' it like—" Larry rubbed his sleeve over his mouth twice before he went on. "While we've got Jamie to think about, we can manage, but when he's packed off somewheres—to learn readin' an' writin' for the blind—an' we're scattered to the four winds o' Ireland, we'll be realizin' for the first time what we are, just. Then what are we goin' to do? I ask ye it honest, miss."

And honestly Sheila answered, "I don't know."

A day later "Granny" whispered over his dressings: "Faith there's a shadow creeping over the sill. Can't ye be feeling it?" And the color-sergeant's spirits failed to rise that day at all.

Yet for all their fears the inevitable day came upon them unawares and caught them, as you might say, red-handed. Sheila had stolen a half-hour from rest and was sitting with them, listening to Casey Ryan, the Galway lad, tell of the fishing in Kilkieran Bay.

Larry took the words out of his mouth. "'Twill be the proud day for us all when we cast our eyes on Irish wather again, whether 'tis in Dublin Bay or off the Skerries."

"Aye, and smelling the thorn bloom and hearing the throstles sing!" "Granny's" rejoicing followed on the heels of Larry's, while he shook his fist at him in warning.

Larry threw a helpless look at Jamie and sank back on his pillow, while Patsy roared his ultimatum: "I'd a deal sight rather hear a throstle sing than see all the bloody wather in the world. Larry's fair mad about wather ever since he went dirty for a fortnight at Vimy."

"Sure, the thing I'm most wantin'," croaked "Bertha," "is to hear the wind in the heather again, deep o' the night. There isn't a sweeter sound than that, so soft an' croony-like."

"Yes, an' I'll be wantin' to hear the old cracked voice o' Biddy Donoghue callin' cockles at the Antrim fair. Faith, she's worth thravelin' far to be hearin'. An' think o' gettin' your tooth on a live cockle!" Johnnie moistened his lips in anticipation as he broke forth in a falsetto:

"Cockles—good cockles—here's some for your dad,
An' some for your lassie—an' more for your lad."

Amid the appreciative chuckle of the listeners, the door of Ward 7-A opened and the chief stood on the threshold. He smiled as a man may when he has a hurting thing to do and grudges the doing of it. He saluted the remnants of Company—of the Royal Irish:

"Orders, lads. You'll be leaving to-morrow for—Blighty."

There was nothing but silence, a silence of agony and apprehension, until Patsy whispered, "Leavin' *together*, sir?"

"I—hope so."

"Thravelin'—the same?" It was Timothy Brennan this time.

"I don't know."

"Will we be afther makin' the same hospital yondther—do ye think?" It took all Larry's fighting soul to keep his voice steady.

"I—It isn't likely."

"Thank ye, sir."

That was all. The chief left, and Sheila sat on in the stillness of Ward 7-A, wondering wherein lay the value of theories when in the face of the first crucial need one sat stunned and helpless. The mask of good spirits had dropped from the lads like a camouflaged screen; behind it showed the naked, bleeding souls of twelve terror-stricken men. For Jamie's mask was still upon him. If the orders had brought any added misery to him, no one could have told.

As Sheila looked into their faces and saw all that was written there, she gripped her hands behind her and tried to tell them what she had thought out so clearly in the operating-room days and days before. But the message she had thought was hers to give had somehow become meaningless. What guarantee had she to make that their lives would go on being vital, necessary to the big scheme of humanity? How could she promise that out of their share in the war and the price they had paid would be wrought something so fine, so strong and eternal, that the years ahead must needs hold plenty for their hearts and souls? She could not get beyond the realization that it was all only theory, the theory of one glowingly healthy mind in a sound body. If such a promise could be given at all, it must not come from such as she; if it was to bear faith, it must be spoken by one who had gone through the crucible as they had gone through—and come out even as they had come.

She looked at Jamie. If Jamie had only had eyes to catch the meaning of the thing she was trying to say! If he who had sung courage into their hearts in the old days could sing it once again! A message from Jamie would bring it home.

But there was nothing in that blank, white face Sheila could reach. He seemed as he had seemed from the beginning, a soul apart, so wrapped in its own despair that no human cry of need could shake it free. In desperation she looked at Larry. His eyes were closed; his face had gone almost as white as Jamie's. Patsy was gazing at the ceiling; the veins on his arms stood out as they had on that first day when he had fainted twice from the pain of his dressing. Down the line of cots the nurse's eyes traveled, and back again. Every lad was past speaking for another; each lay transfixed with his own personal fear.

The minutes seemed intolerable. The silence grew heavy with so much muffling of despair. Sheila found herself praying that the men would groan, cry out, curse, anything to break the ghastly hush. Then suddenly "Bertha" propped himself as best he could on an elbow and croaked: "For the love of Mary, miss, can't ye cram us with morphine the night? 'Twould save the British Empire a few shillin's' expense and them at home a deal o' misery."

And the color-sergeant choked out, "Aye, in God's mercy send us west, along wi' them lucky seven that has gone already!"

Without knowing why she did it, Sheila reached over and gripped one of Jamie's hands. "Help, can't you?" she whispered. The late afternoon sun was shining through the window back of him. The glory of it was full on his face, so that every lad in the ward saw plainly the smile that crept into the lips, a tender, whimsical smile that belonged to the Jamie of old. And the deep, vibrating voice was the voice of the Jamie of fighting days.

"Patsy, ye rascal! I'm thinking it was like yourself to come breaking into the first song I've had on my lips in a month. You've nearly ruined it for me, lad."

Amazement, incredulity, thanksgiving swept over the faces like puffs of wind over young wheat. Unnoticed, Sheila turned to the window and wept a scattering of tears that could no longer be held back. Jamie pulled himself out of the wheel-chair and found his way down the space at the foot of the cots to the door. He was very straight, and his head was high.

"Just a minute, lads." He dug his hands deep into his pockets. "Before I give ye the song I've made for ye, there's something I have to be saying first. Miss O'Leary was right when she said a man has more than one pair of eyes to see with. He can see grand with his heart—if he's shown the way. That's what I have to thank ye for this day, the wiping of my memory clean of those last days, and the showing me how to see anew. Ye've given Ireland back to me with her lark songs, her blue, dancing water, her wind-brushed heather like a purple sea. Ye've made the world beautiful for me again, and ye've given me the heart to sing."

He stopped a minute and smiled again. "I was thinking all this when the chief came in, and after that I was so busy with the song that sprang into my mind that I came near forgetting the lot o' ye. If that rascal Patsy hadn't interrupted me, faith, I might have made the song longer."

Sheila turned back from the window. There was a grin on the face of every lad, and on the face of Jamie was the look of a man who had found his dreams again. The song being new to his tongue, he gave it slowly:

> "They say the earth's a bit shot up—well, we can say the same,
> But, praise to every lad that's fought, the scars they show no shame.
> And for those who have prayed for us—why, here's an end to tears.
> Sure, God can do much healing in the next handful of years.
>
> "So, Johnnie, set your chanter and blow your pipes full strong,
> And, Larry, raise your voice again and lead our marching song.
> Let Mac unfurl the colors—till they sweep yon crimson west,
> For we're still the Royal Irish, a-fighting with the best."

And that is precisely the way they went when they left the American Military Hospital No. 10 the next morning. The color-sergeant led. Jamie walked beside the stretcher to give a hand with the staff. Johnnie sat bolt upright, bolstered with many pillows, to enable him to get a firm grip on the pipes, and he skirled the "Shule Aroon" as he had never skirled before. Larry's voice again boomed in the lead, and every man in the hospital that had breath to spare cheered them as they passed. And for every one who saw or heard the going of the Royal Irish, that day, was left behind a memory green enough to last till the end of time.

Chapter VIII

INTO HER OWN

THE last big drive was on. Somewhere on the road between what had been the line of defense and what was the line of farthest advance rumbled a hospital camion with its nose to the war trail like an old dog on a fresh scent. In the camion sat Sheila O'Leary, late of the old San and later yet of the American Military Hospital No. 10. She was in field uniform; a pair of the chief's own boots were strapped over two pairs of woolen stockings. She was contemplating those boots now with a smile of rare contentment that showed its inwardness even in the gray light of early morning.

"Never thought I should step into the shoes of a great surgeon. They ought to pass me through to the front if everything else fails, don't you think?"

The chief eyed her quizzically. "They'll carry you as far as you'll care to go and for as long as you'll stand. What's troubling me is what your man will say when he knows?"

"Who—Peter?" Sheila's smile deepened. "He'll understand; he'll be glad. Something both of us will remember always, something big to share. Oh, I know it's going to be life and death, heaven and hell, rolled into a minute, but I wouldn't be missing this chance—" She broke off suddenly, and when she spoke again there was a great reverence in her voice. "I feel as the littlest angel might have felt if God had asked him to be at the Creation."

"Rather different, this." Griggs, the chief's assistant, spoke. There were just the three of them in the ambulance.

"Not so very. It's another big primal happening, the hurling together of elemental things and impulses and watching something more solid and lasting come out. A new heaven and a new earth."

"What we see coming out won't be so solid or so lasting. We may not be ourselves." Griggs was a pessimist, a heroic one, with an eye ever keen for the grimmest and most disappointing in life and a courage to meet it squarely.

The chief's glance brushed him on its way to the nurse; Griggs's share of it was plainly commiserating. "And I say, blessed be those who shall inherit it. But, girl, this doesn't settle the question of your man. I've had to duck orders a bit to bring you along. Women aren't wanted at the front. He may hold it up stiff against me for it."

"But I can help. Any woman who can stand it will be needed. They shouldn't bar us out. That's all Peter'll think about. Don't worry."

There was no question in the girl's mind as to the wisdom or right in her coming—or Peter's verdict in the matter. He would not fuss over this plunge into danger any more than he had misunderstood her giving away her wedding back at the old San and coming over at the eleventh hour. The last words Peter had said when he left her for the front came back with absolute distinctness:

"Whatever happens, do what you think best, go where you feel you must go. Don't bungle your instincts. I'd trust them next to God's own."

No, Peter Brooks would have been the last person to deny her this chance, and so all was well. She was wondering now if by some rare good luck she might stumble on Peter at the front. She had not seen him since they separated the day after their arrival in France. A few penciled hieroglyphics had come from time to time telling her all was well with him. She had written when she could and when she knew enough of an address to risk a letter reaching him. But Peter, after the manner of all correspondents, was like Hamlet's ghost—here, there, and gone; and Sheila had no way of knowing if her letters had ever reached him.

For weeks it had seemed to the girl that her love had lain dormant, hushed under the pressure of work. So vital and eternal were both love and happiness that in her zeal for perfect, impersonal service she had thrust them both out of sight, as one might put seeds away in the dark to wait until planting-time, assured of their fulfilment when the time came. But now in the lull between the work at the hospital and the work that would soon claim her again she discovered that in some inexplicable manner love would no longer be shut out. She was sick for the man she loved.

A funny little wistful droop took Sheila's lips, and her chin quivered for an instant. It was so unlike the girl that the chief, seeing, reached across and laid a hand on her knee.

"What is it? Not sorry?"

"Never. But I was thinking how pleasantly easy it might have been to stay behind at the old San. Peter and I'd be climbing that mythical hilltop of ours, with a home of our own at the end of the climb—if we'd stayed behind."

"Well, why didn't you?"

The nurse laughed softly. Griggs volunteered to answer for her.

"Because you were a fool, like a lot of the rest of us."

"Because—oh, because of that queer something inside us all that pries us away from our determinations just to be contented and happy all our lives and hustles us somewhere to do something for somebody else. Remember in the old fairy-tales they were always cleaning the world of dragons or giants or chimeras before they married and lived happy ever after."

"Bosh! Remember that it's only in the fairy-tales that the giants or the monsters don't generally get you, and you get an epitaph instead of a wedding. You romantic idealists make me sick," and Griggs snarled openly.

Their mobile unit was held up that day in a little ruined city. Only one other dressing-station was there, and the wounded were passing through so fast and so wounded that many could not go on. So they set up another dressing-station and worked through the night until the stars went out and their orders came to hurry on. They caught two hours' sleep and by noon of another day they were as close to the front as a hospital unit could go.

A dugout had been portioned out to them, and while orderlies brought in their equipment and the surgeons were coupling up lights and sterilizer, Sheila started to get a hot meal in two sterilizing basins. The nurse was just drawing in her first breath of real war. Before she had time to exhale it a despatch-bearer climbed down into the dugout and handed an order to the chief. It was from headquarters, and brief. The division did not intend to have any woman's name on its casualty list. Sheila was to be returned at once. The bearer added the information that an ambulance was returning with wounded; she could take it.

The chief had never seen the nurse turn so white. Her eyes spoke the appeal her lips refused to make. He tried to put something into words to make it easier for her, but gave it up in final despair. What was there to say? In silence the girl put on her trench coat, jammed on her hat, and was gone. For the first kilometer her senses were too numbed to allow for much thinking. Mechanically she passed her canteen to one of the wounded, readjusted a blanket over another. It was not until the division turned loose its first barrage that day that she woke up to what was happening to her. She was going back; she was not going to have her chance.

The noise was terrific. It drowned everything but the mutinous hammerings of her own heart. In the flash of an eye she changed from the Sheila O'Leary of civilized production to a savage, primitive woman. She had but one dominating instinct, to stand by the male of her tribe, to succor him, fight with him, die with him. It seemed as futile a thing to try to stay this impulse as to try to put out the burning of a prairie when the wind blows.

The ambulance stopped with a jerk. Something was wrong with the engine. The driver climbed down and threw back the hood, and, unnoticed, the nurse slipped down and passed him. When he had finished his tinkering, Sheila was fifty rods away across the meadow.

"Here, you, you come back!" shouted the driver.

For answer Sheila doubled her speed.

The driver watched her, uncertain what to do. A shell whizzed from beyond the barrage and burst a hundred yards from the nurse. The shock threw her, but she was up in an instant, her course changed toward some deserted trenches. The driver hesitated no longer. He climbed back and started the engine.

"No use tacklin' them kind," he remarked to the empty seat beside him. "She'll get there or she won't—but she won't turn back."

It was nightfall when Sheila came up with what she had chosen to call "her division." She intended to possess it in spite of the commander. An outpost sentry challenged what he thought a wraith. His tongue fumbled the words, "Oh, Gawd! it's a woman!"

"Yes. Will you pass her? Lots to do."

He looked at the red cross on her arm and smiled foolishly. "You bet there is! Sure I'll pass you."

She came up with the first battalion, bivouacked under a shell-riven ridge.

"A woman!" The first boy whispered it, and the exclamation rippled on to the next and the next like wind in dry leaves. Remembering the exodus of the morning, the nurse knew if she was to stay she must prove her need and prove it quickly. Her voice was as business-like as in the old San days.

"Dressing-station? Company's surgeon? Wounded? Doesn't matter which, only get me some work."

A hand slipped out of the darkness and caught her elbow. "This way, lady," and she was drawn along the protecting shelter of the ridge. After rods of stumbling she stumbled down irrational stairs into the same dugout she had left that morning. She was almost as surprised as the two surgeons.

"You're a fool," muttered Griggs. "Wait till they order me back. I'll not be crying for purgatory twice."

The chief smiled. "I reckon you got that S O S call I've been sending out all day. We need help like sixty. Bichloride's under that basin. We'll be ready for you when you've washed up. Night ahead—" His words trailed off into an incoherent chuckling. He was wondering how the girl had managed it.

He was wondering more what the command would do when it found out. In the mean time he was glorying in her courage; he would see she got full measure of the work that had claimed her in spite of orders, while he silently thanked a merciful God for providing her.

No one questioned her right to be there that night. Wounded poured in, flooded the dugout to capacity, were cared for, carried away, and more flooded again. It was daybreak before a lull came, and then there were orders to be ready to follow the battalion in an hour. So they ate a snatch, packed, and rolled on in the wake of the Allies' conquest.

Again it was nightfall before they caught up with their regiment. Even to eyes as inexperienced as theirs it was easy to see it had been factored and factored again, and not the half of it was standing. They found a couple of regimental surgeons floundering through a sea of wounded. The nurse had to bite her lips to keep back the cry of horror over the apparent hopelessness of the task that lay before them. So many—and so few hands to do it all!

A shout went up from the men who had come through whole, when they saw her. They were wet, covered with mud, aching in every joint and sinew, but they forgot it all in their joyful pride over the fact that the nurse was standing by.

"Gosh durn it, it's our girl!"

"Stuck fast to the old bat. Whoopee!"

"At-a-boy! Three cheers for the pluckiest girl on the front—our girl!" and a young giant led the cheering that sprang as one yell from those husky throats.

"She's all right—our girl's all right—'rah-'rah-'rah!"

Sheila's own voice was too husky to more than whisper, as she slipped behind the giant, "Tell them my thanks and—good luck."

"You bet I will."

From that instant there was no more helplessness in the feelings of Sheila O'Leary. She felt empowered to move mountains, to make new a mangled heap of boys. As she joined the chief she stopped to see how it was with him. His eyes met hers, and in the flash she read there the same fighting faith that was in her own heart. He patted her shoulder.

"Didn't think you'd funk. Nothing like team-work when you're up against it. Keeps you believing in the divinity of man, eh?"

And who can tell if at times like these the power of the Nazarene does not pass on to those who go fearlessly forth to minister in the face of death! It would not be so strange if he had passed over innumerable battle-fields and so anointed those who had come to succor that their task was made easier and their burden at least bearable.

There was no shelter for any of them that night. They worked in the open, and volunteers came from the ranks to do what they could. The surgeons would have scorned them, but the nurse mustered in a score or more to keep the fires under the kettles burning, to hold supplies and lanterns, to make coffee when the sterilizing basins could be surrendered for the purpose; and she showed those with pocket-knives how to cut away the blood-soaked clothing. Caked with mud herself and desperately hungry, she dressed and comforted as she went. The scene was ghastly—Verestchagin might have painted it—but Sheila saw none of it. It was for her a time exalted, even for those she helped to die. There was no sting in this death. As she passed on and on in the darkness the space about her seemed filled with the shadowy forms of those whom God was mustering out, peacefully, gloriously waiting His command to march into a land of full promise. So acutely did she feel this that a prayer rose to her lips and stayed there, mute, half through the night, that some time she might be given the chance to make this clear for those who mourned at home, to make them feel that death, here, held no sting.

In the midst of it Sheila felt a heavy hand laid on her arm, and turned to look into the face of the commander.

"Are you the nurse I ordered back two days ago?"

"I believe so."

"Who ordered you back again?"

"No one."

"How did you come?"

The girl laughed softly. She could not resist the memory of that flight. "Engine went wrong and I—beat it. Don't blame the driver; he did his best to obey orders. I joined the division last night and came on with my chief."

"So there's no use in ordering you back?"

"None in the least—that is, not so long as the boys are coming in like this."

"How long can you stand it?"

"As long as they can, sir." And then without rhyme or reason tears sprang into the nurse's eyes, to her great mortification and terror. That would probably finish her; a woman who cried had no place at the front, and the general would dismiss her promptly and with scorn.

But he did not. The hand that had touched her arm reached out and gripped her hand. She caught a whimsical smile brushing his lips in the dark.

"Good night. When you want your discharge, I'll sign it."

He went as swiftly and silently as he had come. The nurse turned back to her work with a sigh of relief. The regiment was hers officially now.

The next day they made another little town. So quickly and unexpectedly had the enemy been forced to evacuate it that there had been no time to destroy or pillage, and the shells had somehow passed it by. The town was full of liberated French—the young and very old—who crowded the streets and shouted their welcome as the troops passed through. The chapel was flung open to receive the wounded, and the hospital unit was installed therein.

As Sheila O'Leary crossed the threshold of the little church a strange feeling sprang at her, so that her throat went dry and her heart almost stopped beating. It was as if something apart from her and yet not apart had spoken and said: "Here is where the big moment of your life will be staged. Whatever matters for all time will happen here, and what has gone before—the San, the hospital, everything you have felt, striven for, believed in, and trusted—all that is but a prologue. The real part of your life is just beginning—or—"

Griggs broke the terror that was clutching at her. "What's the matter? Don't you know there's a war going on and about a million wounded coming in? There are a few hundred of them up there, lying round under the images of the saints. The saints may bless 'em, but they won't dress 'em. The chief's growling for you. Come along!"

For once she was grateful to the pessimist. She tried to brush the strangeness away as she hurried down the aisle, but it clung in spite of her. And at the altar more strangeness confronted her. A slightly wounded lad suddenly reached out a hand holding a crumpled paper.

"Guess you're Miss O'Leary, ain't you? He said there wasn't much of a chance, but what you don't expect over here is what you get. You know?"

The incoherency was lost on Sheila. She took the crumpled paper wonderingly and found it covered with Peter's scribbled hieroglyphics:

BELOVED:

The boys have been telling me about you—to think you're really with us and standing by! It may bring its dole of horror—bound to—we all have our turn at it. If it comes, hold to your courage and take deep hold of that wonder-soul of yours; that will steady you. And remember, there is peace coming, and home—yours and mine. Close your eyes when the sights get too bad, and you'll see that blessed house of ours on the hilltop you've chosen; you'll see the little lamp shining us good cheer. Think of that. I'm with the other wing now, but any day I may be shifted to yours. Until then,

Yours,
    "P. B."

The nurse thrust the paper into the front of her uniform, shook the hand that had brought it to her, and passed up the steps to the work that was waiting for her. The first day passed like a dream. Guns boomed, shells screeched their way overhead and landed somewhere. Wounded came and went. Many died, and a white-haired, tottering old sexton helped to carry them away. The old palsied *abbé* came and chanted prayers for the dying, and some one played a *"Dies Iræ"* on the little organ. Old French mothers stole in timorously and offered their services, the service of their hands and emptied hearts. When they found they might help they were pathetically grateful, fluttering down between the aisles of wounded like souls with a day's reprieve from purgatory. They were finding panacea for their bereavement in this care of the sons of other mothers. And as they passed Sheila, in broken sentences, almost inarticulate, they told their sorrow:

"Six—all gone, ma'm'selle."

"Jean, François, Paul, and Victor—Victor the last—he fell two months ago."

"Four sons and four daughters—a rich legacy from my dead husband, ma'm'selle. And I have paid it back—soul by soul—all—he has them all now."

So they mourned as they went their way of tender service, the words dropping unconsciously from their quivering old lips. A few there were who stood apart, the envied mothers with hope. Sheila learned who they were almost from the beginning. Each had a son somewhere not reported. Old Madame d'Arcy whispered about it as she bathed the face of the boy who looked so much like her own.

"Of course, ma'm'selle, my Lucien may be—I have not heard from him in many months. It is not for me to hope too much. But I think—yes, I think, ma'm'selle, he will come home to me when the war is over."

And Madame Simone, who brought fresh black coffee and little cakes for those who could eat them, trembled with the gladness of ministering to the boys who were fighting with hers for France. "I had almost ceased to pray when the Americans came, but now—ah, ma'm'selle, now there is hope again in this withered breast. I even dream now of mon p'tit—the youngest of them all. I feel the good God is sparing him for me."

And old Isabelle, who came to scrub the floor and clean, muttered, as she bent her willing back to the labor: "Moi, that is what I say, too. The Lord will send my Jacques home to comfort my old age."

As Sheila listened, it epitomized for her the tragedy of the mothers of France, this antiphonal chorus of the mothers who had lost all and those who had yet one son left. To the girl's mind there came in almost cruel contrast that chorus of Maeterlinck's mothers raised in rapturous expectancy to the unborn; she knew she was hearing now the agonized antithesis of it. Throughout the first day it rang incessantly, until she could have hummed the haunting melody of it. Then night came. The patches of reds and greens and blues that had sifted through the stained-glass window in the chancel and played all day in grotesque patches on the white cheeks of the wounded faded alike to gray, and the nurse lit the tall wax candles on the altar that the work might go on without stopping.

The next day—and the next—passed much the same. There was no end to the wounded. Griggs fainted twice the second day, and the chief and Sheila carried the work alone for a few hours. Each of them was acutely conscious of the strain on the other and did what he and she could to ease the tension. For the girl her greatest comfort was in the scrap of paper crumpled over her breast. It told her Peter was near, coming to her soon. It seemed to transmit some of his strength and optimism. There were moments when, but for his reassurance, the girl would have doubted every normal, happy phase of life and acknowledged only the unending torture and renunciation. Sometimes the horror seemed to wrap them in like an impenetrable fog. As for the chief, it took every ounce of will and sanity to keep him going, and he wondered how the girl beside him could brave it through without a whimper.

Always about them roared the great guns like the last booming of a judgment day, and under that noise the moaning chorus of the French mothers. When the strain reached the breaking-point Sheila closed her eyes and looked for the light on the hilltop that Peter had promised would be there—and there it always was. Moreover, she could feel Peter's vital presence and the marvelous reality of his love reaching nearer and nearer to her through the darkness. So she kept her head clear and her hands steady and forced a smile whenever the chief eyed her anxiously. She never failed a boy "going west." To the last breath she let him see the radiating faith of her own soul that believed in the ultimate Love above everything else. Those old illuminating smiles that had won for her her nickname of Leerie never had to be forced, and they lighted the way out for many a groping soul in that little church. And the old Frenchwomen, watching above their prayers for the return of Louis or Charles or Jacques, said:

"See, for all she's so young, she knows what the mother-heart is. That is why she feels for us. She knows how our hearts have bled."

On the 9th of November they were still there. The division had continued its drive, but slowly, and no orders had come for the mobile unit to go forward. And then came one of those lulls and flush-backs which for the moment made one almost believe that the tide of battle had turned again—and for the enemy. With the coming of the first wounded that day came orders to evacuate the town at once.

At first the townsfolk would not believe, but as the muddy columns of the first company could be seen on the outskirts, doubt gave place to certainty, and without moan they gathered up what few belongings they could and set their faces toward what they prayed would hold French soil. Before the refugees had cleared the town, the shelling began, giving the last impelling haste to their exodus. The hospital unit stayed in the church. They got the wounded ready to be moved and waited for further orders. They came in another ten minutes; everybody was to clear out. Three ambulances from the east and a half-dozen from the west gathered up the stretcher cases, while the others piled into the supply-trucks—that is, all but the chief and Sheila. They stood in the church door with minds for anything but going. It came to them both that, as the battalions fell back, each would be bringing its wounded as far as it could. If there was a place to drop them—and care waiting until a few more ambulances could push through—many lives might be saved, and much suffering.

The chief looked down at the girl and saw what was in her mind. Linking his arm in hers, he muttered under his breath, "Still game, bless you!" And then aloud: "Miss O'Leary and I have a liking for this place. We'll stay until the next orders."

Griggs had climbed to the footboard of an ambulance, and he faced them with contempt. "We didn't volunteer to sit 'round and be blown to bits. Don't be fools, you two. Come on while you've got a chance." And then, when he saw how futile were his words: "If you haven't had enough slaughter for one while, I have. Good-by."

As they waved them off, the muddy column of the first company swung down the street. It was even as they had thought—wounded were with them, and the nurse and surgeon hurried inside to make ready. The day wound itself out in an almost ludicrous repetition of events. Straggling companies fell back, dropped their wounded, and went on; a few ambulances made the town, gathered up the worst cases, and went back. Desultory shells picked off their belfry, smashed a group of monuments in the cemetery, and wiped out a street of houses not far away. And every half-hour or so came the orders to evacuate at once. Regiment after regiment fell back through the city; the rest of the division must have passed to north and south of it. By nightfall nearly all had passed and the town was left like a delta between two dividing currents.

"They'll begin shelling in earnest by midnight. We'll get barrages from both sides. We won't know it, but this town's going to be wiped off the map tonight." The chief said it in his most matter-of-fact voice, but his face showed gray.

The girl hushed him. "The boys might hear, and they've been through so much. There's no harm in letting them hope." She turned back to the emergency kettle she was stirring. They were making cocoa and feeding the boys out of the chalice-cups from the altar. To the nurse it seemed like passing the last communion, and though her hands kept steady, her heart seemed drained.

Out of the noise and the gathering gloom outside came two more stretcher-loads. The bearers whistled when they saw the red cross on the door. They whistled harder when they pushed it open and looked inside. "Gee! we thought all you outfits had been ordered back!" The bearers laid down their burden on a pew, and the fore one groaned out the words.

"We were," the chief spoke. "Sorry we didn't go?"

"Dunno. Bet these chaps wouldn't be, though—if they knew. Don't know whether it's any use trying; they're all but gone, Doc." The speaker jerked his head over his shoulder and thumbed a command to the other bearers. "Here you, Jake! You and Fritzie hustle along with yours."

As the surgeon bent over to examine, the nurse stopped an instant to listen, then went on feeding her boys.

"This one's French." The chief was looking over the first stretcher. "How did you pick him up?"

"Got mixed up with a company of *poilus* in the last scrap. We fought all together."

"Hmmmm! He'll need speed or he'll make it. Give me a hand with him, boys, over to the table there."

"Wait, Doc. There's another just as bad. He's—the other's a Yank."

The spokesman again jerked his comrades into further evidence. One of the bearers was an American, the other a captured German, slightly wounded. Between them lay a figure in the gray uniform of a correspondent. A heavy growth of beard made the man almost unrecognizable, but something tugged at the chief's memory and set him speculating. He cast a furtive glance over his shoulder toward the nurse, then lowered his voice.

"You haven't any idea who it is, have you?"

"Sure. He's the A. P. man that's been with our division from the first. His name's Brooks."

The chalice fell through Sheila's fingers and struck the altar steps with a sharp, metallic ring. The next instant she was beside the chief, looking down with wide, unbelieving eyes at the stretcher which held nothing familiar but the gray uniform—and there were many men wearing the same. It could not be. This was not the way Peter was coming back to her. In all the days of horror, of caring for the hundreds of wounded, it had never entered her mind that war might claim the man she loved. Her love, and the fulfilment thereof, had stood out as the one absolute reality of life, the thing that could not fail. This simply could not be; Peter was still far away, but coming, supreme in his strength, invulnerable in his love and promise to her.

"You—don't know him?" The chief asked it hopefully.

The girl shook her head. "He can't be—The beard—Wait." Her hand slipped through the opening in his uniform to an inside pocket. She drew out a flat bundle of papers, and the first glance told her all she needed to know. There was Peter's unmistakable scribbling on the uppermost, and from under it showed the corner of one of her letters to him.

The chief's hand steadied her. "No time to lose, girl, but we'll pull him through. We've got to fight for it, but we'll do it. Easy there, boys. Take him over to the table, there, under the light."

But Sheila O'Leary put out a detaining hand. Her eyes were no longer on Peter; she was looking at the figure on the other stretcher. "What did you say about that French boy?"

"He'll have to go, poor chap! There isn't time for both. Listen, Leerie," as a flash of pain swept the girl's face, "it's a toss-up between them who's worse, and it's down now to a matter of minutes. It means the best team-work we've done yet to save just your man."

Still the girl made no move. Her eyes were turned away. In her ears was ringing the chorus of the mothers, those waiting for Louis or Jacques or Lucien to come home. Dear God, what was she to do?

The chief pulled her sleeve. "Wake up, girl. There's a chance for your man, I tell you, only in Heaven's name don't waste it! Come."

She tried to take her eyes away from the boy, tried to shut her ears to the cry that was ringing in them. She wanted to look at Peter and say the word that would start the bearers carrying him to that little zone of light about the altar where they had saved so many during those days. But her eyes clung, in spite of her, to the white boy-face and the faded blue uniform below it. Peter had no mother, no one but herself to face the grief and mourn the loss of him, and the hearts of French mothers had been drained—bled almost to the last drop? Wouldn't Peter say to save that drop? Had she the right to shed it and spare her own heart's bleeding? The questions filtered through her mind with the inevitableness of sands in an hour-glass. With a cry of agony she wrenched her eyes away at last and faced the chief.

"We'll let Peter—wait. We'll take the boy—first."

Dumfounded, the chief stared for the fraction of a moment; then he shook her. "For God's sake, wake up, Leerie! You've gone through so much, your thinking isn't just clear. Get rational, girl. You'd be deliberately killing your man, to leave him now. You don't realize his condition, or you wouldn't be wasting time this way. By the time we finish with the first there'll be no chance for the second; they're both bleeding in a dozen places. Here, boys! Help me over with Mr. Brooks."

But Sheila put out a quick hand and held them back. "And if I put Peter first I shall be deliberately killing the other. Don't you see? I can't do it—Peter wouldn't wish it—it would mean—Boys, carry over the other. The chief's going to save a lad for France."

There was no denying her. She stood guard over Peter's stretcher until the other had been lifted and carried away. Grimly the surgeon followed, and Sheila turned to the two who were still holding the stretcher.

"Would you mind putting him down there? Now, will you leave us just a minute?" She spoke to the American, but the German must have understood, for he led the way to the church door and stood with his back to her.

Even the comfort of staying with Peter to the last was denied her. The chief had said it must be team-work, the best. She mustn't waste many seconds. She thought of the many she had helped to die, the courage a warm grip of the hand had given, the healing strength in a smile, and her heart cringed before this last sacrifice of giving Peter over to a desolate, prayerless death. Hardly breathing, she slipped down and laid her cheek to his bearded one. She could offer one prayer, that he need never wake to know. Kneeling there, his last words came back to her almost in mockery:

"Don't bungle your instincts. I'd trust them next to God's own."

Dear God, if she only could bungle them! If only they had not wrenched from her this torturing, ghastly choice! She knew the meaning now of the strangeness that had met her as she first crossed the threshold of the little church. She knew why the chorus of mothers had been sung so deep into her heart. The greatest moment of her life had come—a terrible, soul-rending moment. And beyond it lay nothing. She choked out an incoherent, futile prayer into the dulled ears—and left him. This—this was her farewell to Peter Brooks—her man—her man for all time.

The American orderly had disappeared. Sheila stumbled over to the door and gripped the sleeve of the German.

"If he opens his eyes"—she opened and shut her own eyes in pantomime—"come for me, quick. Verstehen?"

The German nodded.

For the next half-hour, with nerves keyed to their utmost and hands working with the greatest speed and skill they were capable of, Sheila O'Leary's soul went down into purgatory and stayed there. Not once did she look beyond the boy she was helping to save; not once did she let herself think what might be happening beyond the circle of light that hemmed them in. With all the woman courage she could muster, she was stifling every breath of love or longing—or self-pity. If she could have killed her body and known that when that night's work was done she would be laid in the cemetery outside with Peter, she would have been almost satisfied.

Suddenly she realized they had finished. The chief was repeating something over and over again.

"The boy is safe. You'd better lie down."

The bearers were moving the boy back to the pews and the chief was leading her down the steps of the chancel. But it was Sheila who guided their steps at the bottom. She led the way toward the German and the thing he had been asked to watch. Terror shook her. It seemed as if she could never look at what she knew would be waiting for her, and yet no power on earth could have held her back.

As she reached the prisoner she saw in bewilderment a strange scattering of things on the floor about him—forceps, some knives, a roll of gauze, and a syringe. There was an odor of a strange antiseptic which made her faint. She tottered and would have fallen had the German not helped the chief to steady her.

"He has not gained consciousness, madam. He has lost too much blood for that." The German spoke in English. He also spread his hands in mute apology for what he had done. "I have stanched his wounds with what poor supplies I had with me. It has merely kept him alive. He will require more care, better dressing."

No one answered. Words seemed the most impossible and absurd means of expression just then.

The German smiled at the look Sheila gave him, and the smile was arrogant. "You Americans have always made such a fuss over what you have been pleased to call our brutalities. What is war if it isn't a consistent effort to exterminate the enemy? The women are the wives of the enemy and the breeders of more; the wounded are still the enemy—if they recover, they fight again. But a German knows how to honor a brave act. And when you go back, madam, you can tell how Carl Tiefmann, a German surgeon, wounded and taken prisoner, so far forgot his Prussian creed as to spare an enemy for a brave woman."

He bowed and went back to the church doors. Sheila watched him go through a trailing of mist; then she dropped through the chief's arms, unconscious, on the floor beside Peter's stretcher.

The Germans never reached the little town, and by some merciful stroke of luck neither did any more of the shells. So it came to pass that on the 11th of November a very white nurse, holding fast to the hand of a man unconscious on a stretcher, followed Peace across the threshold of the American Military Hospital No. 10. It was days before Sheila spoke above a husky whisper or smiled, for it was days before Peter was out of danger, but there came a morning at last when a shaven and shorn Peter, looking oddly familiar, opened clear, sane eyes and saw the woman he loved bending close above him.

"He will require more care, better dressing"

He gave the same old cry that he had given ages before when he had come out of another nightmare of unconsciousness and fear, "It's Leerie—why, it's Leerie!"

And Sheila smiled down at him again with the old luminous smile.

When he was sufficiently mended to look about him and take reckoning of what had happened, he asked first for the ring that he had bought for that long-before wedding and that he had carried ever since with him. And he asked, second, for the chaplain.

Sheila drew the gold chain from about her neck and dangled the ring in front of his nose. "I took it when we cut off your coat that night, and I've kept it handy ever since. The chaplain's handy, too. He's promised—any hour of the day or night. Shall we send for him—now?"

Peter nodded.

The nurse turned to go, hesitated, and then came back to the cot. Peter thought he had never seen her eyes so full of wonder.

"Man o' mine, maybe you won't want me when you know I almost let you go, that I intended to let you die to save first a French lad that came in with you."

Peter grinned. "Same old Leerie! Well, we're quits, sweetheart, and I'm glad to have it off my conscience. Sort of did the same thing myself. Rushed off in the shelling to bring in that same poor chap—he'd got a bullet in his leg—and all the time I knew I ought to be thinking of you first and hanging on to safety. Funny, isn't it, how something queer gets you in the midst of it all and you do the last thing in the world you want to do? A year or two and the whole thing will be unexplainable."

Sheila bent over and laid her lips to Peter's. She knew that in a year—in a century—they would still understand why they had done these things, and she was glad they had both paid their utmost for the love and happiness that she knew was theirs now for all time.

Peter broke on her reverie with a chuckle. "Remember old Hennessy saying once that he believed you would give me away with everything else—if you thought anybody else needed me more? He'd certainly wash his hands of the pair of us."

"Hennessy's an old dear. I'll get the chaplain, and afterward let's send Hennessy the first—and the best—cable he's ever had. Sort of owe it to him, don't we?"

Without any of the original splendor of decorations, collation, and attire, with no one but the chaplain to marry them and the chief to bless them, Sheila O'Leary came into her own at last. As for Peter—he looked as Hennessy described him on the day the Brookses came home—"wi' one eye on the thruest lass God ever made an' the other on Paradise."

AFTERWORD

I THOUGHT I had to have a better ending to the story than the scraps of things I had made over from Leerie's letters and what Peter had told me. So I went to Hennessy.

It was midwinter. I found him cracking the ice on the pond to let the swans in for a cold bath.

"'Tis not docthor's ordthers," he grinned by way of explanation; "but they get so blitherin' uneasy there's no housin' them. That's the why I give them a bit of a cold nip onct the while—sure 'tis good threatment for us all—an' then they settle down."

I huddled deeper into a fur coat and tried to agree with Hennessy.

"Did ye see Leerie, then, since she came home?"

"Have you?"

He shirred his lips into an ecstatic pucker and whistled triumphantly. "Wasn't I always sayin' she'd marry the finest gentleman in the land, same as the King o' Ireland's only daughter, and go dandtherin' off to a fine home of her own?"

"And she has."

"She has that."

"And so the story's told, Hennessy."

"Told nothin'. Sure, it isn't half told—it isn't more than half begun, just."

"But you can't end a book that way. You have to end with an ending."

"'Tis the best way to end a book, then. Haven't ye taken the lass over the worst o' the road an' aren't ye leavin' her with the best ahead?"

"But what is there left—to find along the way? She's found her work—that's over with. She's found her man—that's over with. She's found love—that's over—"

Hennessy interrupted me almost viciously. I think he wanted to prod me instead of the ice. "What kind of talkin' is that for a person who thries to write books about real folk? Ye harken to me. Do ye think because love is found 'tis over with? Sure, Leerie's only caught a whiff of it yet—'tis naught but budded for her. By an' by there come the blossom of it an' the fruit of it. An' when death maybe withers it for a spell—'twill be but a winther-time promise to bud an' blossom again in the Counthry Beyond. There's no witherin' to love like hers. An' do ye think because she has her man found there's no pretty fancy or adventure still waitin' them along the way? An' do ye think Leerie's work will ever be done? Tell me that!"

The shirr tightened into something like contempt. Hennessy looked down upon me with undisguised pity.

"Did ye ever know Leerie at all, at all, I'm wondtherin'—to be savin' things like that? Don't ye know for the likes o' her there'll be childher—Saint Anthony send them a nestful!" He crossed himself to further the wish. "An' over an' above the time it takes tendin' an' lovin' them an' rearin' them into the finest parcel o' youngsters God ever made—wi' the help o' their parents—there'll be time left to light the way for every poor, sorry soul within a hundred miles o' her. Ye can take my word for it; an' if she never did another stroke o' work so long as she lived—bein' Leerie, just, would be enough."

"You may be right, Hennessy, but it's still no way to end a book."

He came a step nearer and shook a warning finger at me. "Will ye listen? Faith, I'm wondtherin' sometimes that folk read your books when ye have so little sense wi' the endin' o' them. Don't ye know that a book that ends wi' the end is a dead book entirely? An' who cares to be readin' a dead book? Tell me that."

His contempt changed to commiseration. I might have been Brian Boru, the gray swan, the way he looked at me.

"The right way of endin' is with a beginnin'—the beginnin' o' something bigger an' betther an' sweeter. 'Tis like ye were takin' a friend with ye up a high hill—showin' him all the pretty things along the way. Then just afore ye get to the top—an' afore ye can look over an' see what's waitin' beyond—ye leave him, sayin', 'Go ye alone an' find whatever ye are most wishin' for.'"

He stopped, pushed his hat back and pulled his forelock as if for more inspiration. "Do ye see? Just be leavin' it to folk the world over. They can read in a betther endin' than ye can be writin' in in a hundthred years. An' let Leerie be as I'm tellin' ye—wi' the road windin' over the hill an' out o' sight. Sure the two of us know what she'll be findin' there; an' do ye think the readers have less sense than what we have?"

THE END

CPSIA information can be obtained
at www.ICGtesting.com
Printed in the USA
LVHW040601081222
734780LV00030B/1075